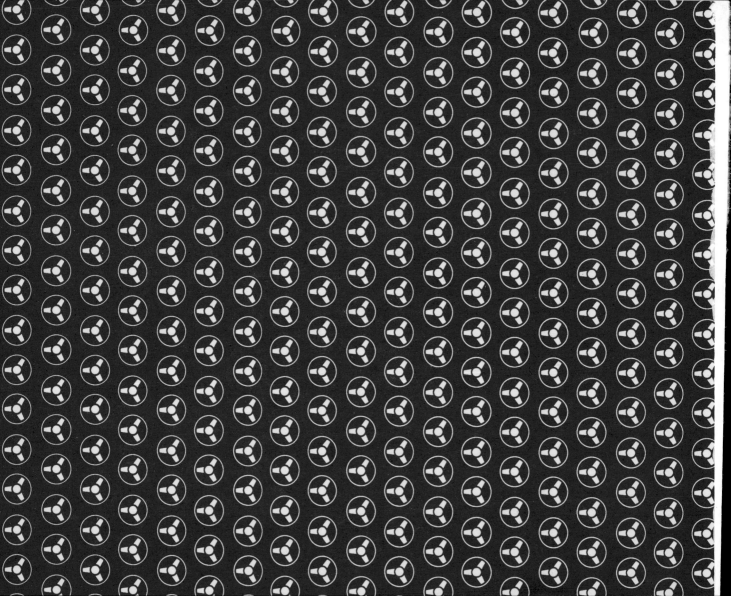

CAR TALES

CAR TALES

CLASSIC STORIES ABOUT DREAM MACHINES

PHOTOGRAPHS BY JANE GOTTLIEB

INTRODUCTION BY MARIO ANDRETTI

VIKING
STUDIO
BOOKS

For Andy, Brindell, David, Frank, Lynn, Sarah,
and my Dad.

VIKING STUDIO BOOKS

Published by the Penguin Group
Viking Penguin, a division of Penguin Books USA Inc., 375 Hudson Street, New York, New York 10014, U.S.A.
Penguin Books Ltd, 27 Wrights Lane, London W8 5TZ, England
Penguin Books Australia Ltd, Ringwood, Victoria, Australia
Penguin Books Canada Ltd, 2801 John Street, Markham, Ontario, Canada L3R 1B4
Penguin Books (N.Z.) Ltd, 182–190 Wairau Road, Auckland 10, New Zealand

Penguin Books Ltd, Registered Offices: Harmondsworth, Middlesex, England

First published in 1991 by Viking Penguin, a division of Penguin Books USA Inc.

10 9 8 7 6 5 4 3 2 1

Copyright © Fly Productions, 1991
Photographs copyright © Jane Gottlieb, 1991
Introduction copyright © Mario Andretti, 1991
All rights reserved

Grateful acknowledgment is made for permission to reprint the following copyrighted works:
 "And These Went Down To Burlington" from *Author's Choice* by MacKinlay Kantor. Copyright 1929 by The Chicago Daily News, renewed © 1957 by MacKinlay Kantor. Reprinted by permission of Mr. Tim Kantor and Mrs. Layne Kantor Shroder.
 "The Family Bus" from *The Price Was High: The Last Uncollected Stories of F. Scott Fitzgerald* by Matthew J. Bruccoli, copyright, 1933 by The Curtis Publishing Company and renewed 1960 by Frances Scott Fitzgerald Lanahan. Reprinted by permission of Harcourt Brace Jovanovich, Inc.
 "Many Miles Per Hour" from *Little Children* by William Saroyan. Copyright 1937 by William Saroyan and renewed 1965 by William Saroyan. Reprinted by permission of The William Saroyan Foundation.
 "Second Chance" from *About Time* by Jack Finney. Copyright © 1986 by Jack Finney. Reprinted by permission of Simon & Schuster, Inc.

Library of Congress Cataloging-in-Publication Data
Car tales : classic stories about dream machines / with photographs by Jane Gottlieb.
     p.   cm.
   Contents: Second chance / by Jack Finney — The family bus / by F. Scott Fitzgerald — And these went down to Burlington / by MacKinley Kantor — Many miles per hour / by William Saroyan — How it happened / by Arthur Conan Doyle.
   ISBN 0-670-83572-2
   1. Automobiles--Fiction.   2. Short stories, American.   I. Gottlieb, Jane.
PS 646.A85C37   1991
813' .0108356--dc20   90-50445
                                                                    CIP

Printed in Singapore

F L Y
PRODUCTIONS

CONTENTS

INTRODUCTION   *vii*
Mario Andretti

THE FAMILY BUS   *1*
F. Scott Fitzgerald

SECOND CHANCE   *45*
Jack Finney

AND THESE WENT DOWN TO BURLINGTON   *69*
MacKinlay Kantor

MANY MILES PER HOUR   *85*
William Saroyan

HOW IT HAPPENED   *97*
Arthur Conan Doyle

MARIO ANDRETTI

Cars are at the center of my life. I am lucky — I am able to enjoy the most sophisticated cars in the world because of what I do. I can use cars to satisfy my moods. One day I may feel like driving my BMW, the next day my Lamborghini, the next day my Corvette. But to drive an Indy car or a Formula One car is to catapult yourself into the ultimate driving experience. I live for this.

Racing for me goes very deep and has gone deep right from the beginning. It caught my fancy long before I was a teenager. I never thought that I would do anything else in my life. I never gave myself the chance to have an alternative. I didn't always know how I would go about it, but somehow I knew I would. It wasn't my father's idea, either. In fact, no one probably had a tougher time convincing his parents that racing was an honorable profession to undertake than myself. My father's big concern, of course, was the safety of my brother Aldo and me. He never tried to understand what drove us. He

didn't talk to us for almost a year when he discovered we were racing regularly — we really tried to hide it from him. He never knew that we did it as much as we did until Aldo was seriously hurt. When he found out, he gave me a serious thrashing — Italian-style.

After Aldo's accident, my father thought we had gotten racing out of our system, that it was settled, end of story. What he didn't know was that while the family was visiting Aldo for eighty days straight in the hospital, I had immediately started building a new car. When Dad learned about the new car, he resigned himself, at last, to the fact that we were going to race no matter what. But he never really accepted it openly. It took a couple of years before Dad could really see what racing did for us. When we started winning, his worry turned to pride.

Jane Gottlieb's dynamic car photographs bring to my mind those individuals who express themselves through automobile design. Compare the sophistication in automobile design these days with the cars of the past. You can see how it has changed dramati-

cally. This is especially visible in the last twenty years. The old design standard was "If you can't do anything else, chrome it." Designers before were not able to create a car with clean lines. How difficult it must have been to design an efficient automobile — aerodynamically and functionally — with style. Sleek, sophisticated designs are commonplace now. I've always admired the skill of the men and women who successfully meet the challenge of shaping an automobile from the ground up.

My first new car was a 1957 Chevrolet. That was my love. At that time, cruising was the thing to do — hardtop, windows down, looking to drag somebody. It was a great way to impress girls — a hot car, a lot of chrome. Today, I can go to a class reunion or a party somewhere and I run across someone from my past, and they still remember, and talk to me about, my '57 Chevy.

Your automobile — the way it looks, the way it drives, the way you use it — can become a reflection of your personality, just like the clothes you wear, the home you live in, or the dog you walk on a Saturday afternoon. Clearly, the authors who have written the car stories in this book were inspired by some very remarkable automobiles, just as I have been.

THE FAMILY BUS

Dick was four years old when the auto arrived at the Hendersons' — it was a 1914 model, fresh from the factory — but his earliest memory of it was dated two years later. Lest younger readers of this chronicle hesitate to embark on an archaeological treatise — about a mummy with doors in the back, gasoline lamps, gears practically in another street, and, invariably, a human torso underneath and a woman all veil and muff perched serene on top — it were best to begin with a description of the vehicle.

This was not that kind of car. It was of an expensive make, low-slung for that period, with electric lights and a self-starter — in appearance not unlike the machines of today. The fenders were higher, the running board longer, the tires more willowy, and undoubtedly it did stick up higher in the air. If it could be stood today beside, say, one of the models of 1927 that are still among us, you would not immediately be able to define the difference. The older car would seem less of a unit — rather like several

F. SCOTT FITZGERALD

——————

cars each on a slightly different level.

This was not apparent to young Dick on the day he became conscious of the car; its sole fault was that it didn't contain Jannekin Melon-Loper, but he was going to make it contain her if his voice held out.

"Why ca' I ha' Ja'kin?"

"Because we're going someplace," his mother whispered; they were approaching the gardener's cottage, and Jan Melon-Loper, father of the coveted Jannekin, tipped his large straw from a grape arbor.

"Oh, waa-a-a!" Dick wailed. "Oh, waa-a-a! I want Ja'kin!"

Mrs. Henderson was a little afraid of the family retainers; she had grown up in a simpler Michigan where the gardener was known either as "the janitor" or "the man who cuts the grass." The baronial splendor made possible by the rise of the furniture company sat uneasily upon her. She feared now that Jan had heard her son's request and would be offended.

"All right," she said, "all right. This one more time, Dick."

He beamed as he ran into the cottage calling for his love; he beamed as, presently, he led her forth by the hand and embarked her at his side. Jannekin, a lovely little Hollander of five, mouthed her thumb shyly for a minute and then found ease in one of those mysterious children's games which consist largely of the word "Look!" followed by long intervals of concentration. The auto carried them far on the fair day, but they gazed neither at the river, nor the hills, nor the residences, but only at each other.

It was always to be the last time with Jannekin, but it never quite was. Dick grew up to ten and played with boys, Jannekin went to public school and played with girls, but they were always like brother and sister to each other, and something more. He told her his most intimate secrets; they had a game they played

sometimes where they stood cheek to cheek for a moment and breathed deeply; it was as near as she would come to letting him kiss her. Once she had seen her older sister kissing a man, and she thought it was "ookey."

So, for the blessed hour of childhood, they eliminated the space between the big house and the small one.

Jannekin never came to the Hendersons'. They met somewhere about the place. Favorite of all rendezvous was the garage.

"This is the way to do," Dick explained, sitting at the gears of the car — it was "the old car" now; the place of honor had since been occupied by a 1917 limousine and a 1920 landaulet — "Look, Janny; look, Jannekin, Howard showed me. I could drive it if they'd let me. Howard let me drive it once on his lap."

"Could I drive it?"

"Maybe," he conceded. "Look, I'll show you how."

"You could drive," she said. "I'd just go along and tell you which way to turn."

"Sure," he agreed, without realizing to what he was committing himself. "Sure, I — "

There was an interruption. Dick's big brother Ralph came into the garage, took a key from behind a door and expressed his desire for their displacement from the machine by pointing briskly at each of them in turn and then emphatically at the cement floor.

"You going riding?" Dick asked.

"Me? No, I'm going to lie under the tank and drink gasoline."

"Where are you going?" asked Dick, as they scrambled out.

"None of your business."

"I mean if you're going out the regular way, would you let us ride as far as Jannekin's house?"

"I can stand it."

He was not pleasant this summer, Dick's brother. He was home from sophomore year at college, and as the city seemed slow, he was making an almost single-handed attempt to speed it up. One of that unfortunate generation who had approached maturity amid the confusions and uncertainties of wartime, he was footloose and irresponsible even in his vices, and he wore the insigne of future disaster upon his sleeve.

The Henderson place was on the East Hills, looking down upon the river and the furniture factories that bordered it. The forty acres were supervised by the resourceful Jan, whose cottage stood in the position of a lodge at the main entrance, and there Ralph stopped the car and, to the children's surprise, got out with them. They lingered as he walked to the gate.

"Tee-hoo!" he whistled discreetly, but imperatively. "Tee-ee-hoo!"

A moment later, Kaethe Melon-Loper, the anxiety, if not yet the shame, of her parents, came around the corner from the kitchen, hatted and cloaked, and obviously trying to be an inconspicuous part of the twilight. She shared with Jannekin only the ruddy Dutch color and the large China-blue eyes.

"Start right off," she whispered. "I'll explain."

But it was too late — the explanation issued from the cottage personified as Mrs. Melon-Loper and Mrs. Henderson making a round of the estate. Both mothers took in the situation simultaneously; for a second Mrs. Henderson hesitated, her eyebrows fluttering; then she advanced determinedly toward the car.

"Why, Ralph!" she exclaimed. "Where are you going?"

Calmly, Ralph blew smoke at his mother.

"I got a date — and I'm dropping Kaethe at a date she's got."

"Why, Ralph!" There was nothing much to add to this remark, which she repeated in a distraught manner. That he was not speaking the truth was apparent in his affected casualness as well as in the shifty, intimidated eyes of the girl sitting beside him. But in the presence of Kaethe's mother, Mrs. Henderson was handicapped.

"I particularly wanted you to be at home tonight," she said, and Mrs. Melon-Loper, equally displeased, helped her with:

"Kaethe, you get yourself out of the auto this minute."

But the car broke into a sound more emphatic than either of their voices; with the cutout open in a resounding "tp!-tp!-tp!" it slid off down the lane, leaving the mothers standing, confused and alarmed, in the yard.

Of the two, Mrs. Melon-Loper was more adequate to the awkward situation.

"It should not be," she pronounced, shaking her head. "Her father will her punish."

"It doesn't seem right at all," said Mrs. Henderson, following her lead gratefully. "I will tell his father."

"It should not be."

Mrs. Henderson sighed; catching sight of the two children, who loitered, fascinated, she managed to assert herself:

"Come home with me, Dick."

"It's only seven," he began to protest.

"Never mind," she said with dilatory firmness. "I need you for something…. Good night, Mrs. Melon-Loper."

A little way down the lane, Mrs. Henderson released on Dick the authority she could no longer wield over her elder son.

"That's the end of that. You're never to play with that dirty little girl again."

"She isn't dirty. She isn't even as dirty as I am."

"You're not to waste your time with her. You ought to be ashamed of yourself."

She walked so fast that he had trouble keeping up.

"Why ought I be ashamed of myself? Look, mamma, tell me. Why ought I be ashamed of myself?"

He sensed that Ralph had no business driving off into the twilight with Kaethe, but himself and Jannekin — that was another matter. There was great domestic commotion about the affair during the next few days; Mr. Henderson raged at Ralph around the library and the latter sat at meals with a silent jeer on his face.

"Believe me, Kaethe would go bigger in New York than most of the stuff that turns out at the country club," he told his father.

"I've made inquiries, and she has a bad reputation with the people she goes with."

"That's O.K. with me," Ralph said. "I think a girl ought to know something about life."

"Is dissipation 'life'? Sometimes I think you've got a bad heart, Ralph. Sometimes I think none of the money I've spent on your outside got through to your insides. I think now I ought to have started you in the factory at seventeen."

Ralph yawned.

"A lot you know about anything except tables and chairs."

For a week, though — due largely to the firmness of Jan — there were no more night rides. Ralph spent his leisure sampling the maiden efforts of pioneer bootleggers, and Dick, accustomed to the disorganization that, during the 20's, characterized so many newly rich families in the Middle West, when there was scarcely a clan without its wastrel or scamp, concerned himself with his own affairs. These included finding out as much about automobiles as Howard, the chauffeur, could find time to tell him, and searching for his Jannekin again across the barriers that had been raised between them. Often he saw her — the flash of a bright little dress far away across the lawn, an eager face on the cottage porch as he drove out with his mother — but the cordon was well drawn. Finally, the urge to hear her voice became so insistent that he decided upon the clandestine.

It was a late August day, with twilight early and the threat of a storm in the air. He shut himself noisily in his room for the benefit of his mother's secretary, part of whose duties consisted of keeping an eye on him in this emergency; then he tiptoed down a back stairs and went out through the kitchen. Circling the garage, he made his way toward the cottage following the low bed of a stream, a route often used in "cops and robbers." His intention was to get as close as possible and then signal Jannekin with a bird call they had practiced, but starting through a high half acre of hay, he stopped at the sound of voices twenty feet ahead.

"We'll take the old bus" — it was Ralph speaking. "We'll get married in Muskegon — that's where some people I know did."

"Then what?" Kaethe demanded.

"I've got a hundred dollars, I tell you. We could go to Detroit and wait for the family to come around."

"I guess they can't do anything after we're married."

"What could they do? They're so dumb they don't even know I flunked out of college in June — I sneaked the notice out of the mail. The old man's weak — that's his trouble. He'll kick, but he'll eat out of my hand."

"You didn't decide this because you had these drinks?"

"I tell you I've thought of it for weeks. You're the only girl I — "

Dick lost interest in finding Jannekin. Carefully he backed out of the path he had made through the hay and returned to the garage to consider. The thing was awful — though Dick's parents were very incompetent as parents in the postwar world that they failed to understand, the symbol of parental authority remained. Scenting evil and catastrophe as he never had in his life, Dick walked up and down in front of the garage in the beginning rain. A few minutes later, he ran for the house with his shirt soaked and his mind made up.

Snitching or not, he must tell his father. But as they went in to dinner, his mother said: "Father phoned he won't be home…. Ralph, why don't you sit up? Don't you think it looks rather bad?"

She guessed faintly that Ralph had been drinking, but she hated facing anything directly.

"S'mustard for the soo-oop," Ralph suggested, winking at Dick; but Dick, possessed with a child's quiet horror, could not give back the required smile.

"If father will only come," he thought. "If father will only come."

During an interminable dinner, he went on considering.

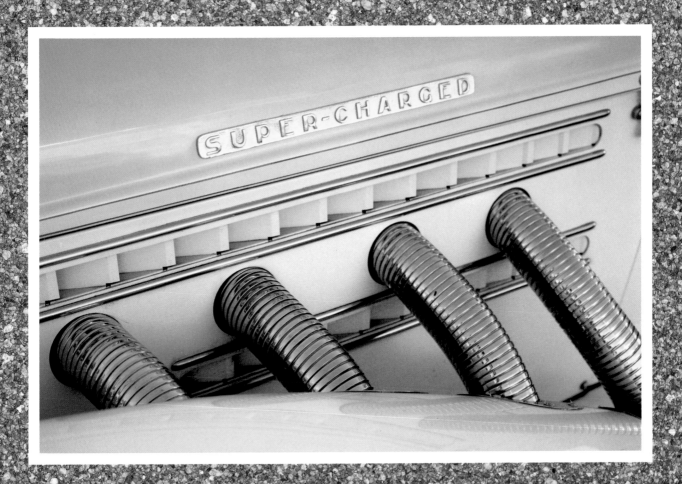

Howard and the new car were in town awaiting his father; in the garage there was only the old bus, and straightway Dick remembered that the key was kept behind the garage door. After a fragmentary appearance in the library to say, "I'm going up and read in my room," he darted down the back stairs again, out through the kitchen and over the lawn, drenched with a steady, patient stream.

Not a second too soon — halfway to the garage he heard the front door close and, by the light of the porte-cochere, saw Ralph come down the steps. Racing ahead, Dick found and pocketed the key; but he ran smack into Ralph as he tried to escape from the garage, and was grabbed in the darkness.

"What you doing here?"

"Nothing."

"Go back the house."

Gratefully, Dick got a start, not toward the house, where he would be easily cornered, but in the direction of the tall hay. If he could keep the key until his father arrived home —

But he had gone barely fifty feet, slipping on the indistinguishable mud, when he heard Ralph's running footsteps behind him.

"Dick, you take 'at key? Hey!"

"No," he called back indiscreetly, continuing to run. "I never saw the key."

"You didn't? Then what were you — "

His fingers closed on Dick's shoulder, and Dick smelled raw liquor as they crashed across a bed of peonies.

"You give me — "

"I won't! You let me — "

"You will, by — "

"I won't — I won't! I haven't got it!"

Two minutes later, Ralph stood up with the key in his hand and surveyed the sobbing boy.

"What was the idea?" he panted. "I'm going to speak to father about this."

Dick took him up quickly.

"All right!" he gasped. "Speak to him tonight!"

Ralph made an explosive sound that expressed at once his disgust and his private conviction that he had best get from home before his father arrived. Still sobbing on the ground, Dick heard the old car leave the garage and start up the lane. It could hardly have reached the sanctuary of a main street when the lights of another car split the wet darkness, and Dick raced to the house to see his father.

"… They're going to Muskegon and they're on their way now."

"It couldn't have been they knew you were there and said it to tease you?"

"No, no, no!" insisted Dick.

"Well, then, I'll take care of this myself…. Turn around, Howard! Take the road to Muskegon, and go very fast." He scarcely noticed that Dick was in the car beside him until they were speeding through the traffic on Canal Street.

Out of the city, Howard had to pick his way more carefully along the wet highway; Mr. Henderson made no attempt to urge him on, but threw cigarette after cigarette into the night and thought his thoughts. But on a down grade when the single light of a motorcycle came into sight on the opposite up grade, he said:

"Stop, Howard! This may be a cop."

The car stopped; owner and chauffeur waved wildly. The motorcycle passed them, pulled up fifty yards down the road, and came back.

"Officer."

"What is it?" The voice was sharp and hurried.

"I'm T. R. Henderson. I'm following an open car with — "

The officer's face changed in the light of his own bright lamp.

"T. R.," he repeated, startled. "Say, I was going to telephone you — I used to work for you. Mr. Henderson, there's been an accident."

He came up closer to the car, put his foot on the running board and took off his cap so that the rain beat on his vivid young face as it twisted itself into sympathy and consideration.

"Your son's car went off the road down here a little way — it turned over. My relief heard the horn keep blowing. Mr. Henderson, you'll have to get ready for bad news."

"All right. Put on your cap."

"Your son was killed, Mr. Henderson. The girl was not hurt."

"My son is killed? You mean, he's dead?"

"The car turned over twice, Mr. Henderson...."

...The rain fell gently through the night, and all the next day it rained. Under the somber skies, Dick grew up suddenly, never again to be irresponsibly childish, trying to make his mother see his own face between herself and the tragedy, voluntarily riding in to call for his father at the office and exhibiting new

interest in the purposes of the mature world, as if to say, "Look, you've got me. It's all right. I'll be two sons. I'll be all the sons you ever would have wanted." At the funeral he walked apart with them as the very cement of their family solidarity against the scandal that accompanied the catastrophe.

Then the rain moved away from Michigan into another weather belt and the sun shone; boyhood reasserted itself, and a fortnight later, Dick was in the garage with Howard while the latter worked on the salvaged car.

"Why can't I look up inside, Howard? You told me I could."

"Get that canvas strip then. Can't send you up to the house with oil on your new clothes."

"Listen, Howard," said Dick, lying under the engine with the basketed light between them. "Is that all it did — broke the front axle? It rolled over twice and only did that?"

"Crawl out and get me that wrench on the table," ordered Howard.

"But why wasn't it hurt?" demanded Dick, returning to the cave. "Why?"

"Built solid," Howard said. "There's ten years' life in her yet; she's better than some of this year's jobs. Though I understand that your mother never wants to see it again — naturally enough."

A voice came down to them from the outside world:

"Dick!"

"It's just Jannekin. Excuse me, Howard; I'll be back and help."

Dick crawled out and faced a little figure in Sunday clothes.

"Hello, Dick."

"What do you want?" he asked, abstractedly rather than rudely; then awakening from mechanical

preoccupations, "Say, who got all dressed up?"

"I came to say good-by — "

"What?"

" — to you."

"Where are you going?"

"We're going away. Father has the van all loaded now. We're going to live across the river and papa's going to be in the furniture business."

"Going away?"

She nodded so far down that her chin touched her breastbone, and she sniffled once.

Dick had restlessly got into the car and was pulling at the dashboard instruments. Suddenly frightened, he flung open the door, saying, "Come here," and, as she obeyed, "Why are you going?"

"After the accident — your father and mine thought we better go away.... Oh-h, Dick!"

She leaned and put her cheek next to his, and gave a sigh that emptied her whole self for a moment. "Oh-h-h-h, Dick! Won't I ever see you?"

For the moment, his only obligation seemed to be to stop her grief.

"Oh, shut up! Stop it, Janny Jannekin. I'll come to see you every day. I will. Pretty soon I'll be able to drive this old bus — "

She wept on inconsolably.

" — and then I'll drive over and — " He hesitated; then made a great concession, "Look, you can drive too. I'll begin to show you now, Janny Jannekin. Look! This is the ignition."

"Yes — hp — oh!" she choked forth.

"Oh, stop it.... Put your foot here. Now press."

She did so, and almost simultaneously a ferocious howl issued from the cavern beneath the car.

"I'm sorry, Howard!" shouted Dick, and then to Jannekin: "But I'll show you how to drive it as soon as they let me take it out myself."

Full in the garage door, the sun fell upon the faces they turned toward each other. Gratefully he saw the tears dry on her cheeks.

"Now I'll explain about the gears," he said.

II

Dick chose Technical High as the best alternative, when it became plain that he could not return to St. Regis. Since Mr. Henderson's death there was always less money for everything, and though Dick resented growing poorer in a world in which everyone else grew richer, he agreed with the trustees that there was not twenty-five hundred extra to send him East to America's most expensive school.

At Tech he thought he had managed to conceal his disappointment politely. But the high-school fraternity, Omega Psi, which, though scarcely knowing him, elected him because of the prestige of his family, became ashamed of their snobbishness and pretended to see in his manner the condescension of a nobleman accepting an election to a fraternal order.

Amid the adjustments of the autumn he did not at first discover that Jannekin Melon-Loper was a junior

in Tech. The thick drift of six years was between them, for she had been right — the separation in the garage was permanent. Jannekin, too, had passed through mutations. Her father had prospered in industry; he was now manager in charge of production in the company that had absorbed the Henderson plant. Jannekin was at Tech for a groundwork that would enable her to go abroad and bring back Bourbon, Tudor, and Hapsburg eccentricities worthy of Michigan reproduction. Jan wanted no more shiftless daughters.

Edgar Bronson, prominent member of Omega Psi, hailed Dick one morning in a corridor. "Hey, rookie, we took you in because we thought you could play football."

"I'm going out for it when — "

"It doesn't do the fraternity any good when you play the East Hill snob."

"What is all this?" demanded Dick, turning on him. "Just because I told some fellows I'd meant to go East to college."

"East—East—East," Edgar accused. "Why don't you keep it to yourself? All of us happen to be headed to Michigan, and we happen to like it. You think you're different from anybody else." And he sang as a sort of taunt:

The boys all are back at Michigan,
The cats are still black at Michigan,
   The Profs are still witty,
      Ha-a-ha!
   The girls are still pretty,

Ha-a-ha! —

He broke off as a trio of girls came around the corridor, and approaching, caught up the song:

— and the old

How do you do?

How are you?

Says who?

Goes on — on — and on.

"Hey, Jannekin!" Edgar called.

"Don't block the sidewalk!" they cried, but Jannekin left the others and came back. Her face escaped the pronounced Dutchiness of her sister's, and the coarseness that sometimes goes with it — nevertheless, the bright little apples of her cheeks, the blue of the Zuyder Zee in her eyes, the braided strands of golden corn on the wide forehead, testified to the purity of her origin. She was the school beauty who let down her locks for the arrival of princes in the dramatic-club shows — at least until the week before the performance, when, to the dismay of the coach, she yielded to the pressure of the times, abbreviated the locks, and played the part in a straw wig.

She spoke over Edgar to Dick, "I heard you were here, Dick Henderson."

"Why" — he recovered himself in a moment — "why, Janny Jannekin."

She laughed.

"It's a long time since you last called me that — sitting in the car in the garage, do you remember?"

"Don't mind me," said Edgar ironically. "Go right on. Did what?"

A wisp of the old emotion blew through Dick, and he concealed it by saying:

"We still have that car. It's still working, but I'm the only person left who can do anything with it when it doesn't."

"What year is it?" demanded Edgar, trying to creep into the conversation that had grown too exclusive to please him.

"Nineteen fourteen," Dick answered briefly and then to Jannekin, with a modesty he did not feel about the car, "We keep it because we couldn't sell it." He hesitated. "Want to go riding some night?"

"Sure I do. I'd love it."

"All right, we will."

Her companions demanded her vociferously down the corridor; when she retreated, Edgar eyed Dick with new interest, but also new hostility.

"One more thing: If you don't want to get the whole fraternity down on you, don't start rushing Jannekin Melon-Loper. Couple of the brothers — I mean she's very popular and there's been plenty fights about her. One guy danced the last number with her at the June dance, and the boy that took her beat him up. Hear that?"

"I hear," answered Dick coldly.

But the result was a resolve that he put into effect during his date with her a week later — he asked her to the Harvest Picnic. Jannekin accepted. Hesitantly, not at all sure she liked this overproud boy out of the past, absorbed in his dual dream of himself and of machinery.

"Why do you want to take me? Because once we were — " She stopped.

"Oh, no," he assured her. "It's just that I like to take the prettiest. I thought we could go in this old bus. I can always get it."

His tone irritated Jannekin.

"I had a sort of engagement to go with two other boys — both of them have new cars." Then, feeling she had gone too far, she added: "But I like this one better."

In the interval he worked over the old bus, touching the worn places of its bright cream color with paint, waxing it, polishing the metal and the glass, and tinkering with the engine until the cutout was calculated to cause acute neurasthenia to such citizenry as dwelt between the city and Reed's Lake. When he called for Jannekin to escort her to the place of assembly, he was prouder of the car than of anything — until he saw whom he was taking to the dance. In deepest rose, a blush upon the evening air, Jannekin bounced rhythmically down the walk, belying the care she had put into her toilet for the night. With his handkerchief he gave a flick to the seat where she was to deposit her spotlessness.

"Good Lord! When I look at you — why, sometimes your face used to be as dirty as mine. Not ever quite — I remember defending you once. Mother said — " He broke off, but she added:

"I know. I was just the gardener's child to her. But why bring that up on an evening like this?"

"I'm sorry. I never thought of you as anything but my Janny Jannekin," he said emotionally.

She was unappeased, and in any case, it was too early for such a note; at the Sedgewicks' house she went from group to group of girls, admiring and being admired, and leaving Dick to stand somewhat conspicuously alone.

Not for long, though. Two youths toward whom he had developed a marked indifference engaged him

in conversation about the football team, conversation punctuated by what seemed to him pointless laughter.

"You looked good at half today, Dick" — a snicker. "Mr. Hart was talking about you afterwards. Everybody thinks that Johnson ought to resign and let you be captain."

"Oh, come on," he said as good-humoredly as possible. "I'm not kidding myself about being good. I know he just needs my weight."

"No, honest," said one of the boys, with mock gravity. "Here at Tech we always like to have at least three of the backfield from the East Hills. It gives a sort of tone to the team when we play Clifton." Whereupon both boys snorted again with laughter.

Dick sighed and shook his head wearily.

"Go on, be as funny as you want to. You think I'm high-hat. All right, go on thinking it until you find out. I can wait."

For a moment, his frankness disconcerted them, but only for a moment:

"And the coach thinks maybe he could use that nifty racer of yours for end runs."

Bored by the childishness of the baiting, he searched for Jannekin in the crowd that now filled the living room and was beginning to drift out to the cars. He saw her flashing rose against a window, but before he could reach her, Edgar Bronson stopped him with serious hands on his shoulders:

"I've got something I particularly want to say to you."

"All right, say it."

"Not here; it's very private. Upstairs in Earl's bedroom."

Mystified, and glancing doubtfully over his shoulder to see if this could be a plot to steal Jannekin away, he followed Edgar upstairs; he refused the cigarette that training did not permit.

"Look here, Dick. Some of us feel that perhaps we've misjudged you. Perhaps you're not such a bad guy, but your early associations with a bunch of butlers and all that stuff sort of — sort of warped you."

"We never had any butlers," said Dick impatiently.

"Well, footmen then, or whatever you call them. It warped you, see?"

Under any conditions it is difficult to conceive of oneself as warped, save before the concave and convex mirrors of an amusement park; under the present circumstances, with Jannekin waiting below, it was preposterous, and with an expression of disgust, Dick started to rise, but Edgar persuaded him back in his chair.

"Wait a minute. There's only one thing wrong with you, and we, some of the fellows, feel that it can all be fixed up. You wait here and I'll get the ones I mean, and we'll settle it in a minute."

He hurried out, closing the door behind him, and Dick, still impatient, but welcoming any crisis that promised to resolve his unpopularity, wandered about the room inspecting the books, school pictures and pennants of Earl Sedgewick's private life.

Two minutes passed — three minutes. Exploding into action, he strode out of the door and down the stairs. The house was strangely silent, and with quick foreboding, he took the last stairs six at a time. The sitting room was unpopulated, the crowd was gone, but there was Jannekin, a faithful but somewhat sulky figure, waiting by the door.

"Did you have a good sleep?" she asked demurely. "Is this a picnic or a funeral?"

"It was some cuckoo joke. Some day I'll pull something on those guys that'll be really funny. Anyhow, I know a short cut and we'll beat them to the lake and give them the laugh." They went out. On the veranda, he stopped abruptly; his car — his beautiful car — was not where he had left it.

"My gosh! They've taken it! They took my car! What a dirty trick!" He turned incredulously to Jannekin. "And they knew you were with me too! Honestly, I don't understand these guys at all."

Neither did Jannekin. She had known them to behave cruelly or savagely; she had never known them to visit such a stupid joke on a popular girl. She, too, stared incredulously up and down the street.

"Look, Dick! Is that it down there — beyond the third lamppost?"

He looked eagerly.

"It certainly is. But why — "

As they ran toward it, the reason became increasingly clear — startlingly clear. At first it seemed only that the car was somehow different against the late sunset; then the difference took form as varicolored blotches, screaming and emphatic, declaratory and exclamatory, decorating the cream-colored hulk from stem to stern, until the car seemed to have become as articulate and vociferous as a phonograph.

With dawning horror, he read the legends that, one by one, swam into his vision:

PARDON MY SILK HAT

WHAT AM I DOING IN THIS HICK TOWN?

ONLY FOUR CYLINDERS, BUT EACH ONE WITH A FAMILY TREE

STRAIGHT GAS FROM THE EAST HILLS

MARNE TAXI — MODEL 1914

WHY BALLOON TIRES WITH A BALLOON HEAD?

And perhaps the cruelest cut of all:

YOU DON'T NEED A MUFFLER WITH A CULTIVATED VOICE

Wild with rage, Dick pulled out his handkerchief and dabbed at one of the slogans, making a wide blur through which the sentence still showed. Three or four of them must have worked on the mural; it was amazing, even admirable, that it had been accomplished in the quarter hour they had passed in the house. Again he started furiously at it with the already green blob of his handkerchief. Then he spied the convenient barrel of tar with the help of which they had finished the job after the paint gave out, and he abandoned all hope.

"There's no use, Dick," Jannekin agreed. "It was a mean trick, but you can't do anything about it now. You'll just ruin your clothes and make it all splotchy and give them the satisfaction of thinking you've been working on it. Let's just get in and go." And she added with magnanimity, "I don't mind."

"Go in this?" he demanded incredulously. "Why I'd sooner — "

He stopped. Two years ago he would have phoned the chauffeur or rented another car, but now dollars were scarce in his family; all he could muster had gone into cosmetics for the machine.

"We can't go," he said emphatically. "Maybe I can find you a ride out and you can come back with someone else."

"Nonsense!" Jannekin protested. "Of course, we'll go. They're not going to spoil our evening with such a stupid stunt!"

"I won't go," he repeated firmly.

"You will so." She reverted unconsciously to the tone of six years before. "By the time we get there, it'll be almost too dark to read the — to see the things they painted. And we don't have to take streets where there're many people."

He hesitated, rebelling with her at being triumphed over so easily.

"Of course, we could go on the side streets," he admitted grudgingly.

"Of course, Dick." She touched his arm. "Now don't help me in; I don't want to get in the paint."

"When we're there," Dick told himself grimly, "I'll ask Mr. Edgar Bronson aside for a little talk. And I'll do some painting myself — all in bright red."

She sensed his fury as they drove along dusty roads with few street lights, but great roller-coaster bumps at the crossings.

"Cheer up, Dick!" She moved closer. "Don't let this spoil the evening. Let's talk about something else. Why, we hardly know each other. Listen, I'll tell you about me; I'll talk to you as frankly as we used to talk. We're almost rich, Dick. Mother wants to move to a bigger house, but father's very cautious, and he thinks it would look pushing. But anyhow we know he's got more than we know he's got — if you know what I mean."

"That's good." He matched her frankness. "Well, we've got even less money than people know we have, if you know what I mean. I've got as much chance of getting East to Boston Tech as this car has to get into th automobile show." A little bitterly, he added: "So they needn't have wasted all that sarcasm."

"Oh, forget it. Tell me what you are going to do."

"I'm not going to college at all; I'm going to Detroit, where my uncle can get me a place in a factory. I

like fooling around cars. As a matter of fact — " In the light of recent happenings, he hesitated before he boasted, but it came with an irrepressible rush: "Over at Hoker's garage they phone me whenever they get a job that sticks them — like some new foreign car passing through. In fact — "

Again he hesitated, but Jannekin said, "Go on."

" — in fact, I've got a lot of little gadgets at home, and some of them may be worth patenting after I get up to Detroit. And then maybe I'll think of some others."

"I'll bet you will, Dick," she agreed. "You could always mend anything. Remember how you started that old music box that father brought from the old country? You — you shook it or something."

He laughed, forgetting his temper.

"That was a brilliant hunch — young Edison in the making. However, it won't work with cars, because they usually shake themselves."

But when the picnic grounds came into sight, at first faintly glowing with many Japanese lanterns upon the twilight, then alive with bright dresses, a hard mood descended upon him. He saw a knot of boys gather at his approach, and looking straight ahead, he drove past the crowd that milled about the laden tables and to the parking place beyond. Voices followed them:

"Who'd have thought it?"

"Must be some Eastern custom."

"Say, that's some jazzy little tank now."

As he swung the car savagely into an empty space, Jannekin's hand fell on his taut arm.

"What are you going to do, Dick?"

"Why, nothing," he answered innocently.

"You're not going to make a scene about this. Wait! Don't get out yet. Remember, you're with me."

"I'll remember that. Nothing'll happen around you."

"Dick, do you know who did this?"

"I know Edgar Bronson had something to do with it. And two others I'm pretty sure of, and — "

"Listen…. Please don't get out, Dick." It was the soft voice of pleading childhood. "Listen, Dick. You could beat any of those three boys, couldn't you?"

"Beat them!" he repeated scornfully. "I could mop up the lake with them. I could ruin any two of them together, and they know it. I'm just wondering what part of the grounds they're hiding in — or maybe they're keeping their girls with them for protection."

He laughed with his chin up, and in the sound there was a wild foretaste of battle and triumph that frightened her and thrilled her.

"Then what would be the satisfaction, Dick?" she begged. "You know already you could beat them, and they know it, and everybody knows it. Now, if it was Capone Johnson — " This was an unfortunate suggestion; she stopped herself too late as lines appeared between Dick's eyes.

"Maybe it was Capone Johnson. Well, I'll just show him he's not so big that he can — "

"But you know it wasn't him," she wailed. "You know he's the kindest boy in school and wouldn't hurt anybody's feelings. I heard him say the other day he liked you 'specially."

"I thought he did," he said, mollified.

"Now we're going to get out and take our baskets and walk over as if nothing had happened."

He was silent.

"Come on, Dick; do it for Janny. You've done so many things for Janny."

Had she put it the other way — that she had done so many things for him — he would not have yielded, but the remark made it seem inevitable that he should do one more.

"All right." He laughed helplessly, but his laugh changed to an intake of breath as, suddenly, her young body pressed against him, all that rose color crushing up to his heart, and he saw her face and eyes swimming under him where the wheel had been a minute before.

A minute later, perhaps even two, even three minutes later, she was saying:

"Let me get out by myself. Remember the paint." And then: "I don't care if I am mussed. At least none of them can say they've seen me so mussed before."

Hand in hand, with that oddly inimitable, not-to-be-masked expression on both their faces, they walked toward the tables beside the lake.

III

But after a few months during which Dick laced up Jannekin's skating boots or kissed her lips in the many weathers of the long Michigan winter, they arrived at another parting.

Jannekin, borne up on the wings of the family fortune, was taken from Tech and sent to be fashionably educated in Europe.

There were forget-me-nots, but after a time there were fewer letters. Jannekin in Geneva, Jannekin in

Paris, Jannekin in Munich; finally Jannekin at The Hague, being presented to the Queen of Holland — Miss Melon-Loper, the gardener's daughter, a splendid plant of the Netherlands that had taken root in the new world.

Meanwhile there was Dick in overalls, Dick with his face grease black, Dick with his arm in a sling and part of a little finger gone. Now, after five years, there was Dick at twenty-three, assistant to the factory superintendent of one of the largest automobile plants in Detroit. Finally, there was Dick driving to his native city, partly on business and partly because word had reached him that Jannekin had once more set foot upon the shore of the republic. The news came through Edgar Bronson, who worked in a competing factory, but was more in touch with home than Dick. Dick wrote, and in return got a telegram inviting him to dine.

They were waiting for him on the porch of a big Dutch-colonial house — not old Jan, who had broken down under the weight of years and been put in a nursing home, but Mrs. Melon-Loper, a stout patroon now, and proud of the family fortunes, and a scarcely recognizable Jannekin, totally unlike the girl who had lost her voice cheering at the game with Clifton or led her basketball team in bloomers. She wasn't merely developed, she was a different person. Her beauty was as poised and secure as a flower on a strong stem; her voice was cool and sure, with no wayward instruments in it that played on his emotions. The blue eyes that pretended a polite joy at their reunion succeeded in conveying only the face value of the eyes them- selves, even a warning that an intention of being amused lay behind them.

And the dinner was like too many other dinners; a young man and woman whose names Dick associated with the city's older families talked cards, golf, horses, country-club scandal; and it became evident to Dick

that Jannekin herself preferred the conversation to remain on a thin, dehumanized level.

"After Detroit, we must sound provincial, Dick." He resented the irony. "But we happen to like it here, really. It's incredible, but we do. We have almost everything, but it's all in miniature. We even have a small version of a hunt club and a small version of the depression — only we're a little afraid at the moment that the latter's going to eat up the former. Nevertheless, Mr. Meredith here isn't any less of an M. F. H. because he has two pairs of boots compared to some Meadowbrook nabob with a dozen."

"Jannekin's subsidized by the Chamber of Commerce." Meredith said. "Personally, I think the place is a ditch, but she keeps arranging and rearranging things until we all think we're in Paris."

She was gone. Dick might have expected that. Once they had recaptured the past after a lapse of six years; it was too much to expect that it would happen again. There was nothing left of the Jannekin he had known, and he was not impressed with her as the ringmaster of the local aristocracy. It was even obvious that she was content to be top dog here because of a lingering sense of inferiority at having been born a servant's daughter.

Perhaps to another man her new qualities would have their value, but she was of no use to him anymore. Before the end of the evening, he had dismissed her from his mind except as a former friend, viewed in enlightening perspective. But he went down the steps empty-hearted from the riddance of that face drifting between the dark and the windows.

Jannekin said, "Come over often, Dick."

With forced heartiness, Dick answered:

"I'm certainly going to!" And to himself he added, "But not to see you, my dear." He did not guess that

she was thinking: "Why did I do this tonight? Whatever made me think he'd like it?"

On his way to the hotel, he stopped by the entrance to his old home. It was unoccupied and for sale. Even with part of the property converted into a real-estate development, there were few families in the city who could undertake its upkeep. Dick sighed, expressing he knew not what emotion.

Down at the hotel he could not sleep. He read a magazine for a while and then bent a long, fine piece of wire that he often carried with him into a shape that might someday be embodied in a spring. Once more he recapitulated to himself the impossibility of loving a girl for the third time, when she was not even the girl he had loved before; and he pictured himself with scorn as one of those faithful swains who live perennially in an old hope from sheer lack of imagination. He said aloud: "This thing is out of my mind for good." And it seemed to vanish obediently and he felt better; but he was not yet quite asleep at two o'clock when the phone pounded at his bedside. It was long distance from Detroit.

"Dick, I want to begin by telling you about McCaffray."

"Who is this speaking?"

"This is Bill Flint calling from the office. But first I want to ask you: Were your father's initials T. R.?"

"What is this, anyhow?" Dick grumbled. "Are you having a party over there?"

"I told you I'm in my office in the drafting building and I've got a stack of files in front of me two yards high."

"This is a fine time of the night — "

"Well, this is a damn important business."

"My father's initials? He didn't know an automobile from a velocipede."

"Shut up and I'll tell you the dope. Now, this McCaffray — "

Back in 1914, a pale little man named McCaffray had appeared in Detroit from nowhere, lingered a few weeks and then inconspicuously died. The little man had had a divine foresight about dual carburetion fourteen years in advance of its time. The company experimentally installed his intake manifolds on the first six cars of a series, abandoned the idea, and let Mr. McCaffray, with his unpatented scheme, wander off to a rival factory and thence on to his death. But within the last twenty-four hours it had become highly important to the company engineers to find out exactly what that intake manifold had looked like. One old mechanic remembered it hazily as having been "something like you want." Apparently no drawing of it was in existence. But though five of the six cars had been issued to company executives and long ago vanished, the sixth had gone out on a hurry order to a certain Mr. T. R. Henderson.

"He was my father," Dick interrupted. "The car is here, laid up in a garage kept by an old chauffeur of ours. I'll have the intake manifold tomorrow."

The family bus again — he felt a rush of sentimentality about it. He'd never sell it; he'd put it in a special museum like the coaches at Versailles. Thinking of it warmly, affectionately, he drowsed off at last, and slept until eleven in the morning.

Two hours later, having accomplished the business that had brought him to the city, he drove to Howard's garage and found him filling a gas tank in front.

"Well, there, Dick!" Howard hurried over, wiping his hands on a ball of waste. "Say, we were talking about you. Hear they made you czar of the auto industry."

"No, only mayor…. Say, Howard, is the old car still running?"

"What car?"

"The old open bus."

"Sure. She never was any five-and-ten proposition."

"Well, I'm going to take her to Detroit." At Howard's expression, he stiffened with alarm. "She's here, isn't she?"

"Why, we sold that old car, Dick. Remember, you told me if I had an offer I could sell it for the storage."

"My God!"

"We got — let's see — we got twenty-two fifty, I think, because the rubber and the battery — "

"Who did you sell it to?"

Howard scratched his head, felt his chin, hitched his pants.

"I'll go ask my daughter how much we did get for it."

"But who bought it?" Dick was quivering with apprehension lest the company of Edgar Bronson, where Mr. McCaffray once labored, had snatched the thing from under his nose.

"Who?" he demanded fiercely.

"Jannekin Melon-Loper bought it."

"What?"

"Sure thing. She came down a month ago, and had to have that car. If you wait a second, I'll ask my daughter — "

But Dick was gone. Had he not been so excited he would have regarded the time and not rung the door-bell at the Melon-Lopers' before a luncheon party of women had risen from the table. As it was, Jannekin

came out on the porch and made him sit down.

"I know you don't want to meet a lot of women, but I'm glad you came, Dick. I'm sorry about last night. I was showing off, I guess."

"Not at all."

"Yes, I was — and in such an idiotic way. Because at dinner it kept running through my head that once your mother had called me a dirty little girl."

He breathed in her sparkling frankness like a draught of fresh air and, as they laughed together, he liked her terrifically again.

"Jannekin, I want to see you soon; we have lots of the past to talk about, you and I. But this is a business call. Jannekin, I want to buy back that old car of ours."

"You knew I had it, then," she said guiltily. "I hated to think of it sitting there so — so aged and so neglected."

It was their old love she was talking about, and he knew it, but she hurried on:

"I hear about you sometimes — from Edgar Bronson. He's done very well, hasn't he? He came down last week and dropped in on me."

Dick frowned, with a resurgence of his old sense of superiority.

"Of all the boys who were at Tech, you two are most spoken of," went on Jannekin innocently.

"Well" — his voice held a touch of impatience — "I musn't keep you from your luncheon."

"That doesn't matter. About the car — if you want it, you can have it, of course. I'll tell the chauffeur to run it around."

A minute later she reappeared, wearing an expression of distress.

"The chauffeur says it's gone. He hasn't seen it for weeks."

Dick turned cold inside.

"It's gone?"

"It must have been stolen. You see, I never bought it to use, but only — "

"This is extraordinary," he interrupted. "I really have to have that car. It's of the greatest importance."

At his change of tone, she hardened also:

"I'm sorry. I don't see what I can do about it."

"Can I look around in back myself? It might be behind the garage or somewhere."

"Certainly."

Scarcely aware of his own rudeness, Dick plunged down the steps and around the house. Wild suspicions surged through him — that Edgar Bronson had persuaded her to part with the car, and now Jannekin, ashamed, was lying to him. It was hard to imagine anyone stealing such an automobile; he searched every foot of the place as if it were something that might be concealed behind a doghouse. Then, baffled and raging, he retraced his steps and stopped suddenly within the range of a sentence that drifted out the kitchen window:

"She ask me, but I wan't goin' to tell her. The old man sell it to me last week with a old gun and fishing tackle, just 'fore they took him down to that institarium. He not givin' nothin' away. So I pay him eight dollar out of my wages and I sell the car to Uncle Ben Govan over to Canterbury for ten dollar. No, suh. Old man sold me that stuff fair and square, and I pay him for it. I just shet my mouth when Miss

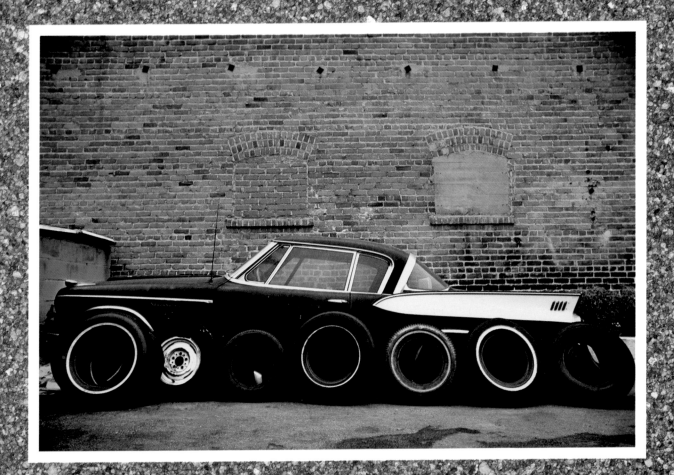

Jannekin ask me. I don't tell her nothin'*at* all."

Dick walked firmly in at the kitchen door. Observing the look in his eye, the chauffeur sprang to his feet, a cigarette dropping from his mouth. A few minutes later, Dick rounded the house again, sorry for his wild imaginings. Jannekin was on the veranda speeding a guest; impulsively, he walked up to her and declared:

"I'm going on an expedition, Janny Jannekin, and you're coming with me right away."

She laughed lightly: "These Motor Boys — he mistakes me for a spare part." But as he continued to regard her, she gave a startled sigh and the color went up in her transparent cheeks.

"Well, very well. I don't suppose my guests will mind. After all, they've been telling me for months I ought to have a young man…. Go in and break the news, Alice, will you? Say I'm kidnaped — try to get the ransom money together."

Pulled not so much by Dick's hand as by his exuberance, they flew to his car. On the way, across the river and up the hill to the darky settlement, they talked little, because they had so much to say. Yassuh, Uncle Ben Govan's house was that one down there. And in the designated hollow a dark, villainous antique came toward them, doffing, so as to speak, his corncob pipe. After Dick had explained his mission and assured him that they were not contesting his legal rights to the machine, he agreed to negotiate. "Yassuh, I got her roun' back. How much you want pay for her, boss?…

"Boss, she's yours." Carefully he requested and pocketed the money, and then led them round to where, resting beside a chicken coop, lay the familiar, cream-colored body of the family bus — cushions, door handles, dashboard and all.

"But where's the chassis?" Dick exploded.

"Chassis?"

"The engine, the motor, the wheels!"

"Oh, that there part." The old man chuckled belittlingly. "That part I done soe a man. This here comfortable part with the cushions, it kept kind of easin' off the wheels when the man was takin' it away, so he lef' it here, and I thought I'd take these cushions and make me two beds for my grandchildren. You don't want to buy it?"

Firmly Dick retrieved ten of the twelve dollars, and after much recapitulation of local geography, he obtained the location of a garage and an approximation of its name.

"The thing sits quiet for five years," he complained as they raced back down the hill, "and then, at the age of about ninety, it begins to bounce around the country like a jumping bean!"

Finally they saw it. It stood in a row of relics back of the garage — a row which a mechanic was about to slaughter.

But one of them was not a junk to Dick and Jannekin as they rushed forward with reprieve in their eyes. There it was, stripped to its soul: four wheels, a motor, a floorboard — and a soap box.

"Take it away for twenty-five," agreed the proprietor, "as it stands. Say, you know, for a job nineteen years old, the thing runs dandy still."

"Of course, it does!" Dick boasted as they climbed on and set the motor racing. "I'm turning in my car on the trade."

"That's a joke!" called back the practical Jannekin as they drove away. "We'll be around for it."

They throbbed down Canal Street, erect and happy on the soap box, stared at curiously by many eyes.

"Doesn't it run well?" he demanded.

"Beautifully, Dick." She had to sit very close to him on the box. "You'll have to teach me to drive, dear. Because there isn't any back part."

"We always sat in the front. Once I consoled you beside this wheel and then once you consoled me — do you remember?"

"Darling!"

"Where'll we go?"

"To heaven."

"By George, I think it'll make it!"

Proud as Lucifer, the flaming chariot swept on up the street.

SECOND CHANCE

I can't tell you, I know, how I got to a time and place no one else in the world even remembers. But maybe I can tell you how I felt the morning I stood in an old barn off the county road, staring down at what was to take me there.

I paid out seventy-five dollars I'd worked hard for after classes last semester — I'm a senior at Poynt College in Hylesburg, Illinois, my home town — and the middle-aged farmer took it silently, watching me shrewdly, knowing I must be out of my mind. Then I stood looking down at the smashed, rusty, rat-gnawed, dust-covered, old wreck of an automobile lying on the wood floor where it had been hauled and dumped thirty-three years before — and that now belonged to me. And if you can remember the moment, whenever it was, when you finally got something you wanted so badly you dreamed about it — then maybe I've told you how I felt staring at the dusty mass of junk that was a genuine Jordan Playboy.

You've never heard of a Jordan Playboy, if

JACK FINNEY

45

you're younger than forty, unless you're like I am; one of those people who'd rather own a 1926 Mercer convertible sedan, or a 1931 Packard touring car, or a '24 Wills Sainte Claire, or a '31 air-cooled Franklin convertible — or a Jordan Playboy — than the newest two-toned, '56 model made; I was actually half sick with excitement.

And the excitement lasted; it took me four months to restore that car, and that's fast. I went to classes till school ended for the summer, then I worked, clerking at J. C. Penney's; and I had dates, saw an occasional movie, ate and slept. But all I really did — all that counted — was work on that car; from six to eight every morning, for half an hour at lunchtime, and from the moment I got home, most nights, till I stumbled to bed, worn out.

My folks live in the big old house my dad was born in; there's a barn off at the back of the lot, and I've got a chain hoist in there, a workbench, and a full set of mechanic's tools. I built hot rods there for three years, one after another; those charcoal-black mongrels with the rear ends up in the air. But I'm through with hot rods; I'll leave those to the high-school set. I'm twenty years old now, and I've been living for the day when I could soak loose the body bolts with liniment, hoist the body aside, and start restoring my own classic. That's what they're called; those certain models of certain cars of certain years which have something that's lasted, something today's cars don't have for us, and something worth bringing back.

But you don't restore a classic by throwing in a new motor, hammering out the dents, replacing missing parts with anything handy, and painting it chartreuse. "Restore" means what it says, or ought to. My Jordan had been struck by a train, the man who sold it to me said — just grazed, but that was enough to flip it over, tumbling it across a field, and the thing was a wreck; the people in it were killed. So the right rear wheel

and the spare were hopeless wads of wire spokes and twisted rims, and the body was caved in, with the metal actually split in places. The motor was a mess, though the block was sound. The upholstery was rat-gnawed, and almost gone. All the nickel plating was rusted and flaking off. And exterior parts were gone; nothing but screw holes to show they'd been there. But three of the wheels were intact, or almost, and none of the body was missing.

What you do is write letters, advertise in the magazines people like me read, ask around, prowl garages, junk heaps and barns, and you trade, and you bargain, and one way or another get together the parts you need. I traded a Winton name plate and hubcaps, plus a Saxon hood, to a man in Wichita, Kansas, for two Playboy wheels, and they arrived crated in a wooden box — rusty, and some of the spokes bent and loose, but I could fix that. I bought my Jordan running-board mats and spare-wheel mount from a man in New Jersey. I bought two valve pushrods, and had the rest precision-made precisely like the others. And — well, I restored that car, that's all.

The body shell, every dent and bump gone, every tear welded and burnished down, I painted a deep green, precisely matching what was left of the old paint before I sanded it off. Door handles, windshield rim, and every other nickel-plated part, were restored, renickeled, and replaced. I wrote eleven letters to leather supply houses all over the country, enclosing sample swatches of the cracked old upholstery before I found a place that could match it. Then I paid a hundred and twelve dollars to have my Playboy reupholstered, supplying old photographs to show just how it should be done. And at eight ten one Saturday evening in July, I finally finished; my last missing part, a Jordan radiator cap, for which I'd traded a Duesenberg floor mat, had come from the nickel plater's that afternoon. Just for the fun of it, I put the old plates

back on then; Illinois license 11,206, for 1923. And even the original ignition key, in its old leather case — oiled and worked supple again — was back where I'd found it, and now I switched it on, advanced the throttle and spark, got out with the crank, and started it up. And thirty-three years after it had bounced, rolled and crashed off a grade crossing, that Jordan Playboy was alive again.

I had a date, and knew I ought to get dressed; I was wearing stained dungarees and my dad's navy blue, high-necked old sweater. I didn't have any money with me; you lose it out of your pockets, working on a car. I was even out of cigarettes. But I couldn't wait, I had to drive that car, and I just washed up at the old sink in the barn, then started down the cinder driveway in that beautiful car, feeling wonderful. It wouldn't matter how I was dressed anyway, driving around in the Playboy tonight.

My mother waved at me tolerantly from a living room window, and called out to be careful, and I nodded; then I was out in the street, cruising along, and I wish you could have seen me — seen *it*, I mean. I don't care whether you've ever given a thought to the wonderful old cars or not, you'd have seen why it was worth all I'd done. Draw yourself a mental picture of a simple, straight-lined, two-seater, open automobile with four big wire wheels fully exposed, and its spare on the back in plain sight; don't put in a line that doesn't belong there, and have a purpose. Make the two doors absolutely square; what other shape should a door be? Make the hood perfectly rounded, louvered at the sides because the motor needs that ventilation. But don't add a single unnecessary curve, jiggle, squiggle, or porthole to that car — and picture the radiator, nothing concealing it and pretending it doesn't exist. And now see that Playboy as I did cruising along, the late sun slanting down through the big old trees along the street, glancing off the bright nickel so that it hurt your eyes, the green of the body glowing like a jewel. It was beautiful, I tell

you it was beautiful, and you'd think everyone would see that.

But they didn't. On Main Street, I stopped at a light, and a guy slid up beside me in a great big, shining, new '57 car half as long as a football field. He sat there, the top of the door up to his shoulders, his eyes almost level with the bottom of his windshield, looking as much in proportion to his car as a two-year-old in his father's overcoat; he sat there in a car with a pattern of chrome copied directly from an Oriental rug, and with a trunk sticking out past his back wheels you could have landed a helicopter on; he sat there for a moment, then turned, looked out, and smiled at *my* car!

And when I turned to look at him, eyes cold, he had the nerve to smile at *me*, as though I were supposed to nod and grin and agree that any car not made day before yesterday was an automatic side-splitting riot. I just looked away, and when the light changed, he thought he'd show me just how sick his big four-thousand-dollar job could make my pitiful old antique look. The light clicked, and his foot was on the gas, his automatic transmission taking hold, and he'd already started to grin. But I started when he did, feeding the gas in firm and gentle, and we held even till I shot into second faster than any automatic transmission yet invented can do it, and I drew right past him, and when I looked back it was me who was grinning. But still, at the next light, every pedestrian crossing in front of my car treated me to a tolerant understanding smile, and when the light changed, I swung off Main.

That was one thing that happened; the second was that my date wouldn't go out with me. I guess I shouldn't blame her. First she saw how I was dressed, which didn't help me with her. Then I showed her the Jordan at the curb, and she nodded, not even slightly interested, and said it was very nice; which didn't help her with me. And then — well, she's a good-looking girl, Naomi Weygand, and while she didn't exactly

put it in these words, she let me know she meant to be seen tonight, preferably on a dance floor, and not waste her youth and beauty riding around in some old antique. And when I told her I was going out in the Jordan tonight, and if she wanted to come along, fine, and if she didn't — well, she didn't. And eight seconds later she was opening her front door again, while I scorched rubber pulling away from the curb.

I felt the way you would have by then, and I wanted to get out of town and alone somewhere, and I shoved it into second, gunning the car, heading for the old Cressville road. It used to be the only road to Cressville, a two-lane paved highway just barely wide enough for cars to pass. But there's been a new highway for fifteen years; four lanes, and straight as a ruler except for two long curves you can do ninety on, and you can make the seven miles to Cressville in five minutes or less.

But it's a dozen winding miles on the old road, and half a mile of it, near Cressville, was flooded out once, and the concrete is broken and full of gaps; you have to drive it in low. So nobody uses the old road nowadays, except for four or five farm families who live along it.

When I swung onto the old road — there are a lot of big old trees all along it — I began to feel better. And I just ambled along, no faster than thirty, maybe, clear up to the broken stretch before I turned back toward Hylesburg, and it was wonderful. I'm not a sports-car man myself, but they've got something when they talk about getting close to the road and into the outdoors again — the way driving used to be before people shut themselves behind great sheets of glass and metal, and began rushing along superhighways, their eyes on the white line. I had the windshield folded down flat against the hood, and the summer air streamed over my face and through my hair, and I could see the road just beside and under me flowing past so close I could have touched it. The air was alive with the heavy fragrances of summer darkness, and

the rich nostalgic sounds of summer insects, and I wasn't even thinking, but just living and enjoying it.

One of the old Playboy advertisements, famous in their day, calls the Jordan "this brawny, graceful thing," and says, "It revels along with the wandering wind and roars like a Caproni biplane. It's a car for a man's man — that's certain. Or for a girl who loves the out of doors." Rich prose for these days, I guess; we're afraid of rich prose now, and laugh in defense. But I'll take it over a stern sales talk on safety belts.

Anyway, I liked just drifting along the old road, a part of the summer outdoors and evening, and the living country around me; and I was no more thinking than a collie dog with his nose thrust out of a car, his eyes half closed against the air stream, enjoying the feeling human beings so often forget, of simply being a living creature. "'I left my love in Avalon,'" I was bawling out at the top of my lungs, hardly knowing when I'd started, "'and saaailed awaaay!'" Then I was singing "Alice Blue Gown," very softly and gently. I sang, "Just a Japanese Saaandman!," and "Whispering," and "Barney Google," the fields and trees and cattle, and sometimes an occasional car, flowing past in the darkness, and I was having a wonderful time.

The name "Dempsey" drifted into my head, I don't know why — just a vagrant thought floating lazily up into my consciousness. Now, I saw Jack Dempsey once; six years ago when I was fourteen, my dad, my mother, and I took a vacation trip to New York. We saw the Empire State Building, Rockefeller Center, took a ride on the subway, and all the rest of it. And we had dinner at Jack Dempsey's restaurant on Broadway, and he was there, and spoke to us, and my dad talked to him for a minute about his fights. So I saw him; a nice-looking middle-aged man, very big and broad. But the picture that drifted up into my mind now, driving along the old Cressville road, wasn't that Jack Dempsey. It was the face of a young man not a lot older than I was, black-haired, black-bearded, fierce and scowling. Dempsey, I thought, that snarling young face

rising up clear and vivid in my mind, and the thought completed itself: He beat Tom Gibbons last night.

Last night; Dempsey beat Gibbons *last night* — and it was true. I mean it *felt* true somehow, as though the thought were in the very air around me, like the old songs I'd found myself singing, and suddenly several things I'd been half aware of clicked together in my mind. I'd been dreamily and unthinkingly realizing that there were more cars on the road than I'd have expected, flowing past me in the darkness. Maybe some of the farm families along here were having some sort of Saturday-night get-together, I thought. But then I knew it wasn't true.

Picture a car's headlights coming toward you; they're two sharp beams slicing ahead into the darkness, an intense blue-white in color, their edges as defined as a ruler's. But these headlights — two more sets of them were approaching me now — were different. They were entirely orange in color, the red-orange of the hot filaments that produced them; and they were hardly even beams, but just twin circles of wide, diffused orange light, and they wavered in intensity, illuminating the road only dimly.

The nearer lights were almost upon me, and I half rose from my seat, leaning forward over the hood of the Jordan, staring at the car as it passed me. It was a Moon; a cream-colored nineteen-twenty-two Moon roadster.

The next car, those two orange circles of wavering light swelling, approached, then passed, as I stared and turned to look after it. It looked something like mine; wire wheels, but with the spare on a side mount, and with step plates instead of running boards. I knew what it was; a Haynes Speedster, and the man at the wheel wore a cloth cap, and the girl beside him wore a large pink hat, coming well down over her head, and with a wide brim all around it.

I sat moving along, a hand on the wheel, in a kind of stunned ecstatic trance. For now, the Saturday-night traffic at its peak, there they all came one after another, all the glorious old cars; a Saxon Six black-bodied touring car with wood-spoke wheels, and the women in that car wore chin-length veils from the edges of their flowered hats; there passed a gray-bodied black-topped Wills Sainte Claire with orange disc wheels, and the six kids in it were singing "Who's Sorry Now?" then I saw another Moon, a light blue open four-seater, its cutout open, and the kid at the wheel had black hair slicked back in a varnished pompadour, and just glancing at him, you could see he was on his way to a date; now there came an Elcar, two Model T Fords just behind it; then a hundred yards back, a red Buick roadster with natural-wood spoke wheels; I saw a Velie, and a roadster that was either a Noma or a Kissel, I couldn't be sure; and there was a high-topped blue Dodge sedan with cut flowers in little glass vases by the rear doors; there was a car I didn't know at all; then a brand-new Stanley Steamer, and just behind it, a wonderful low-slung 1921 Pierce-Arrow, and I knew what had happened, and where I was.

I've read some of the stuff about Time with a capital T, and I don't say I understand it too well. But I know Einstein or somebody compares Time to a winding river, and says we exist as though in a boat, drifting along between high banks. All we can see is the present, immediately around us. We can't see the future just beyond the next curve, or the past in the many bends in back of us. But it's all there just the same. There — countless bends back, in infinite distance — lies the past, as real as the moment around us.

Well, I'll join Einstein and the others with a notion of my own; just a feeling, actually, hardly even a thought. I wonder if we aren't barred from the past by a thousand invisible chains. You can't drive into the past in a 1957 Buick because there are no 1957 Buicks in 1923; so how could you be there in one? You can't

drive into 1923 in a Jordan Playboy, along a four-lane superhighway; there are no superhighways in 1923. You couldn't even, I'm certain, drive with a pack of modern filter-tip cigarettes in your pocket — into a night when no such thing existed. Or with so much as a coin bearing a modern date, or wearing a charcoal-gray and pink shirt on your back. All those things, small and large, are chains keeping you out of a time when they could not exist.

But my car and I — the way I felt about it, anyway — were almost *rejected* that night, by the time I lived in. And so there in my Jordan, just as it was the year it was new, with nothing about me from another time, the old '23 tags on my car, and moving along a highway whose very oil spots belonged to that year — well, I think that for a few moments, all the chains hanging slack, we were free on the surface of Time. And that moving along that old highway through the summer evening, we simply *drifted* — into the time my Jordan belonged in.

That's the best I can do, anyway; it's all that occurs to me. And — well, I wish I could offer you proof. I wish I could tell you that when I drove into Hylesburg again, onto Main Street, that I saw a newspaper headline saying, PRESIDENT HARDING STRICKEN, or something like that. Or that I heard people discussing Babe Ruth's new home-run record, or saw a bunch of cops raiding a speakeasy.

But I saw or heard nothing of the sort, nothing much different from the way it always has been. The street was quiet and nearly empty, as it is once the stores shut down for the weekend. I saw only two people at first; just a couple walking along far down the street. As for the buildings, they've been there, most of them, since the Civil War, or before — Hylesburg's an old town — and in the semidarkness left by the street lamps, they looked the same as always, and the street was paved with brick as it has been since World War I.

No, all I saw driving along Main Street was — just little things. I saw a shoe store, its awning still over the walk, and that awning was striped; broad red and white stripes, and the edges were scalloped. You just don't see awnings like that, outside of old photographs, but there it was, and I pulled over to the curb, staring across the walk at the window. But all I can tell you is that there were no open-toed shoes among the women's, and the heels looked a little high to me, and a little different in design, somehow. The men's shoes — well, the toes seemed a little more pointed than you usually see now, and there were no suede shoes at all. But the kids' shoes looked the same as always.

I drove on, and passed a little candy and stationery shop, and on the door was a sign that said, *Drink Coca-Cola,* and in some way I can't describe the letters looked different. Not much, but — you've seen old familiar trademarks that have gradually changed, kept up to date through the years, in a gradual evolution. All I can say is that this old familiar sign looked a little different, a little old-fashioned, but I can't really say how.

There were a couple of all-night restaurants open, as I drove along, one of them The New China, the other Gill's, but they've both been in Hylesburg for years. There were a couple of people in each of them, but I never even thought of going in. It seemed to me I was here on sufferance, or by accident; that I'd just drifted into this time, and had no right to actually intrude on it. Both restaurant signs were lighted, the letters formed by electric light bulbs, unfrosted so that you could see the filaments glowing, and the bulbs ended in sharp glass spikes. There wasn't a neon sign, lighted or unlighted, the entire length of the street.

On West Main I came to the Orpheum, and though the box office and marquee were dark, there were a few lights still on, and a dozen or so cars parked for half a block on each side of it. I parked mine directly

across the street beside a wood telephone pole. Brick pavement is bumpy, and when I shut off the motor, and reached for the hand brake — I don't know whether this is important or not, but I'd better tell it — the Jordan rolled ahead half a foot as its right front wheel settled into a shallow depression in the pavement. For just a second or so, it rocked a little in a tiny series of rapidly decreasing arcs, then stopped, its wheel settled snugly into the depression as though it had found exactly the spot it had been looking for — like a dog turning around several times before it lies down in precisely the right place.

Crossing over to the Orph, I saw the big posters in the shallow glass showcases on each side of the entrance. *Fri., Sat., and Sun.,* one said, and it showed a man with a long thin face, wearing a monocle, and his eyes were narrowed, staring at a woman with long hair who looked sort of frightened. GEORGE ARLISS, said the poster, in "The Green Goddess."

Coming Attraction, said the other poster, *Mon., Tues., and Wed.* "Ashes of Vengeance," starring NORMA TALMADGE and CONWAY TEARLE, with WALLACE BEERY. I've never heard of any of them, except Wallace Beery. In the little open lobby, I looked at the still pictures in wall cases at each side of the box office; small, glossy, black and white scenes from the two movies, and finally recognized Wallace Beery, a thin, hand-some, young man. I've never seen that kind of display before, and didn't know it was done.

But that's about all I can tell you; nothing big or dramatic, and nothing significant, like hearing some-one say, "Mark my words, that boy Lindbergh will fly the Atlantic yet." All I saw was a little, shut-down, eleven-o'clock Main Street.

The parked cars, though, were a Dort; a high, straight-lined Buick sedan with wood wheels; three Model T's; a blue Hupmobile touring car with blue and yellow disc wheels; a Winton; a four-cylinder Chevrolet

roadster; a Stutz; a spoke-wheeled Cadillac sedan. Not a single car had been made later than the year 1923. And this is the strange thing; they looked *right* to me. They looked as though that were the way automobiles were supposed to look, nothing odd, funny, or old-fashioned about them. From somewhere in my mind, I know I could have brought up a mental picture of a glossy, two-toned, chromium-striped car with power steering. But it would have taken a real effort, and — I can't really explain this, I know — it was as though modern cars didn't really exist; not yet. *These* were today's cars, parked all around me, and I knew it.

I walked on, just strolling down Main Street, glancing at an occasional store window, enjoying the incredible wonder of being where I was. Then, half a block or so behind me, I heard a sudden little babble of voices, and I looked back and the movie was letting out. A little crowd of people was flowing slowly out onto the walk to stand, some of them, talking for a moment; while others crossed the street, or walked on. Motors began starting, the parked cars pulling out from the curb, and I heard a girl laugh.

I walked on three or four steps maybe, and then I heard a sound, utterly familiar and unmistakable, and stopped dead in my tracks. My Jordan's motor had caught, roaring up as someone advanced the spark and throttle, and dying to its chunky, revving-and-ticking-over idle. Swinging around on the walk, I saw a figure, a young man's, vague and shadowy down the street, hop into the front seat, and then — the cutout open — my Jordan shot ahead, tires squealing, down the street toward me.

I was frozen; I just stood there stupidly, staring at my car shooting toward me, my brain not working; then I came to life. It's funny; I was more worried about my car, about the way it was treated, than about the fact that it was being stolen. And I ran out into the street, directly into its path, my arms waving, and I yelled, "Hey! Take it easy!" The brakes slammed on, the Jordan skidding on the bricks, the rear end sliding

sideways a little, and it slowed almost to a stop, then swerved around me, picking up speed again, and as I turned, following it with my eyes, I caught a glimpse of a girl's face staring at me, and a man my age at the wheel beside her, laughing, his teeth flashing white, and then they were past, and he yelled back, "You betcha! Take it easy; I always do!" For a moment I just stood staring after them, watching the single red taillight shrinking into the distance; then I turned, and walked back toward the curb. A little part of the movie crowd was passing, and I heard a woman's voice murmur some question; then a man's voice, gruff and half angry, replied, "Yeah, of *course* it was Vince; driving like a fool as usual."

There was nothing I could do. I couldn't report a car theft to the police, trying to explain who I was, and where they could reach me. I hung around for a while, the street deserted once more, hoping they'd bring back my car. But they didn't, and finally I left, and just walked the streets for the rest of the night.

I kept well away from Prairie Avenue. If I was where I knew I was, my grandmother, still alive, was asleep in the big front bedroom of our house, and the thirteen-year-old in my room was the boy who would become my father. I didn't belong there now, and I kept away, up in the north end of town. It looked about as always; Hylesburg, as I've said, is old, and most of the new construction has been on the outskirts. Once in a while I passed a vacant lot where I knew there no longer was one; and when I passed the Dorsets' house where I played as a kid with Ray Dorset, it was only half built now, the wood of the framework looking fresh and new in the dark.

Once I passed a party, the windows all lighted, and they were having a time, noisy and happy, and with a lot of laughing and shrieks from the women. I stopped for a minute, across the street, watching; and I saw figures passing the lighted windows, and one of them was a girl with her hair slicked close to her head, and

curving down onto her cheeks in sort of J-shaped hooks. There was a phonograph going, and the music —
it was "China Boy" — sounded sort of distant, the orchestration tinny, and . . . different, I can't explain
how. Once it slowed down, the tones deepening, and someone yelled, and then I heard the pitch rising
higher again as it picked up speed, and knew someone was winding the phonograph. Then I walked on.

At daylight, the sky whitening in the east, the leaves of the big old trees around me beginning to stir, I
was on Cherry Street. I heard a door open across the street, and saw a man in overalls walk down his steps,
cut silently across the lawn, and open the garage doors beside his house. He walked in, I heard the motor
start, and a cream and green '56 Oldsmobile backed out — and I turned around then, and walked on
toward Prairie Avenue and home, and was in bed a couple of hours before my folks woke up Sunday
morning.

I didn't tell anyone my Jordan was gone; there was no way to explain it. Ed Smiley, and a couple other
guys, asked me about it, and I said I was working on it in my garage. My folks didn't ask; they were long
since used to my working on a car for weeks, then discovering I'd sold or traded it for something else to
work on.

But I wanted — I simply had to have — another Playboy, and it took a long time to find one. I heard of
one in Davenport, and borrowed Jim Clark's Hudson, and drove over, but it wasn't a Playboy, just a Jordan,
and in miserable shape anyway.

It was a girl who found me a Playboy; after school started up in September. She was in my Economics IV
class, a sophomore I learned, though I didn't remember seeing her around before. She wasn't actually a
girl you'd turn and look at again, and remember, I suppose; she wasn't actually pretty, I guess you'd have to

say. But after I'd talked to her a few times, and had a Coke date once, when I ran into her downtown —
then she was pretty. And I got to liking her; quite a lot. It's like this; I'm a guy who's going to want to get
married pretty early. I've been dating girls since I was sixteen, and it's fun, and exciting, and I like it fine.
But I've just about had my share of that, and I'd been looking at girls in a different way lately; a lot more
interested in what they were like than in just how good-looking they were. And I knew pretty soon that this
was a girl I could fall in love with, and marry, and be happy with. I won't be fooling around with old cars all
my life; it's just a hobby, and I know it, and I wouldn't expect a girl to get all interested in exactly how the
motor of an old Marmon works. But I would expect her to take some interest in how I feel about old cars.
And she did — Helen McCauley, her name is. She really did; she understood what I was talking about, and
it wasn't faked either, I could tell.

So one night — we were going to the dance at the Roof Garden, and I'd called for her a little early, and
we were sitting out on her lawn in deck chairs killing time — I told her how I wanted one certain kind of
old car, and why it had to be just that car. And when I mentioned its name, she sat up, and said, "Why,
good heavens, I've heard about the Playboy from Dad all my life; we've got one out in the barn; it's a beat-
up old mess, though. Dad!" she called, turning to look up at the porch where her folks were sitting. "Here's
a man you've been looking for!"

Well, I'll cut it short. Her dad came down, and when he heard what it was all about, Helen and I never
did get to the dance. We were out in that barn, the old tarpaulin pulled off his Jordan, and we were looking
at it, touching it, sitting in it, talking about it, and quoting Playboy ads to each other for the next three
hours.

It wasn't in bad shape at all. The upholstery was gone; only wads of horsehair, and strips of brittle old leather left. The body was dented, but not torn. A few parts, including one headlight, and part of the windshield mounting, were gone, and the motor was a long way from running, but nothing serious. And all the wheels were there, and in good shape, though they needed renickeling.

Mr. McCauley gave me the car; wouldn't take a nickel for it. He'd owned that Jordan when he was young, had had it ever since, and loved it; he'd always meant, he said, to get it in running order again sometime, but knew he never would now. And once he understood what I meant about restoring a classic, he said that to see it and drive it again as it once was, was all the payment he wanted.

I don't know just when I guessed, or why; but the feeling had been growing on me. Partly, I suppose, it was the color; the faded-out remains of the deep green this old car had once been. And partly it was something else, I don't know just what. But suddenly — standing in that old barn with Helen, and her mother and dad — suddenly I knew, and I glanced around the barn, and found them; the old plates nailed up on a wall, 1923 through 1931. And when I walked over to look at them, I found what I knew I would find; 1923 Illinois tag 11,206.

"Your old Jordan plates?" I said, and when he nodded, I said as casually as I could, "What's your first name, Mr. McCauley?"

I suppose he thought I was crazy, but he said, "Vincent. Why?"

"Just wondered. I was picturing you driving around when the Jordan was new; it's a fast car, and it must have been a temptation to open it up."

"Oh, yeah." He laughed. "I did that, all right; those were wild times."

"Racing trains; all that sort of thing, I suppose?"

"That's right," he said, and Helen's mother glanced at me curiously. "That was one of the things to do in those days. We almost got it one night, too; scared me to death. Remember?" he said to his wife.

"I certainly do."

"What happened?" I said.

"Oh" — he shrugged — "I was racing a train, out west of town one night; where the road parallels the Q tracks. I passed it, heading for the crossroad — you know where it is — that cuts over the tracks. We got there, my arms started to move, to swing the wheel and shoot over the tracks in front of that engine — when I knew I couldn't make it." He shook his head. "Two three seconds more; if we'd gotten there just two seconds earlier, I'd have risked it, I'm certain, and we'd have been killed, I know. But we were just those couple of seconds too late, and I swung that wheel straight again, and shot on down the road beside that train, and when I took my foot off the gas, and the engine rushed past us, the fireman was leaning out of the cab shaking his fist, and shouting something, I couldn't hear what, but it wasn't complimentary." He grinned.

"Did anything delay you that night," I said softly, "just long enough to keep you from getting killed?" I was actually holding my breath, waiting for his answer.

But he only shook his head. "I don't know," he said without interest. "I can't remember." And his wife said, "I don't even remember where we'd been."

I don't believe — I really don't — that my Jordan Playboy is anything more than metal, glass, rubber and paint formed into a machine. It isn't alive; it can't think or feel; it's only a car. But I think it's an

especial tragedy when a young couple's lives are cut off for no other reason than the sheer exuberance nature put into them. And I can't stop myself from feeling, true or not true, that when that old Jordan was restored — returned to precisely the way it had been just before young Vince McCauley and his girl had raced a train in it back in 1923 — when it had been given a second chance; it went back to the time and place, back to the same evening in 1923, that would give them a second chance, too. And so again, there on that warm July evening, actually there in the year 1923, they got into that Jordan, standing just where they'd parked it, to drive on and race that train. But trivial events can affect important ones following them — how often we've all said: If only this or that had happened, everything would have turned out so differently. And this time it did, for now something was changed. This time on that 1923 July evening, someone dashed in front of their car, delaying them only two or three seconds. But Vince McCauley, then, driving on to race along beside those tracks, changed his mind about trying to cross them; and lived to marry the girl beside him. And to have a daughter.

I haven't asked Helen to marry me, but she knows I will; after I've graduated, and got a job, I expect. And she knows that I know she'll say yes. We'll be married, and have children, and I'm sure we'll be driving a modern hardtop car like everyone else, with safety catches on the doors so the kids won't fall out. But one thing for sure — just as her folks did thirty-two years before — we'll leave on our honeymoon in the Jordan Playboy.

AND THESE WENT DOWN TO BURLINGTON

Once the trees and poles stood still for a long time; among the trees was a cluster of purple flowers that stretched friendly tongues to her. She climbed up and stood, hammering both hands against the glass and saying, "Pretty, pretty."

In the front seat, Nanna heard her. "Yes, honeybunch. Pretty. Does baby want a flower?"

"Pretty."

Doddy was out in the road beside the car. He had a funny stick in his hands and he bent over it, making it go up and down steadily. Sometimes he would lift his face and see Gwen looking out at him; if he noticed her he might wink and shake his head briskly…. She would chuckle when he did that.

Other cars went past, but Gwen had seen a great many other cars that day and the day before, so she didn't notice them much. Finally one stopped — it was almost like a large chunk of the sky, it was so blue. Gwen almost wished that she was riding in a car like that. But she was very

MACKINLAY KANTOR

comfortable with Nanna and Doddy. They had a thick, soft cloth thing — it had been taken off the bed at home — and it covered the whole back seat and the mound of suitcases. The baby could crawl around on there without much chance of her getting hurt....

A big man got out of the bright blue car.

"Need any help, brother?"

"Thanks. I'll get it all right."

"Thought maybe you wanted a patch."

"I got one here I think'll hold."

"Okay. Where you headed for?"

"Burlington."

The big man had yellow hair like Gwen's doll. He walked past the windows of the little car; he smiled at Nanna and tapped on the glass with something bright.

"How old's baby?"

"Nineteen months," said Nanna.

Gwen wasn't watching the big man. For in his car was a Wow. She hadn't noticed it before. The Wow sat up very straight inside the blue car and stared at Gwen. She beat on the glass ecstatically and cried, "Wow — Wow!"

The Wow noticed her. He made a sharp, pleasant noise and lifted his ears higher.

"She sees the dog," said the big man. "Well, so long."

"So long. Sure much obliged."

The big car went away suddenly — man and Wow and all. Gwen scrambled across the soft cushions and gazed out of the rear window. She could see the Wow looking back at her…. Maybe it would come again.

Doddy opened the door and slid a lot of sharp, heavy things under the mattress, beside the suitcases. Gwen reached down and tried to get them.

"No, no."

"No?"

"No…. Agnes, make her let those tools alone…. You'll get all dirty, skeezix."

He climbed into the front seat and sat very quietly for a moment. Gwen crept up behind him and breathed softly against his neck. He had on a woolly sweater, much like hers, only it was a brighter color and had holes in it. She put her finger into one of the holes; it was enjoyable to put her finger in, and then pull it out quickly, pretending that the hole was hot-boo.

"Well, kid, that's that."

"Oh, Joe. I sure hope we don't have any more punctures."

"So do I."

"Gosh, honey, what'd we do if we had to buy another tire before we got to Burlington?"

"I dunno…. Don't worry, kid. That old casing's good for a long ways yet."

Then the trees and fences started off again. The purple flowers brushed the side of the car and began to wave at Gwen. So she waved her hand and called loudly, "Bye…."

"Didja hear that, Joe?"

"What?"

"She was waving bye-bye."

He grinned. "What at?"

"Oh…you know. Just waving."

Gwen put her head down on the soft mattress, and watched the trees going past…the motion of the car went through her body with a warm, comfortable ripple, and she stretched out in the softness, watching Nanna and Doddy with quiet gray eyes.

"She's getting sleepy, Joe."

"Huh?"

"Sleepy. The baby's getting — "

"Say, she ain't had anything to eat yet. Not since morning."

"I know it. But she'll take her nap first, and feel lots better. Riding makes them sleepy…."

Gwen heard them saying all this: she heard "eat" and wanted to rouse up and ask, "Crackaw?" But the motion of the car kept rippling in her mind; the world was all purple flowers and big blue cars, and filled with nice Wows which made friendly noises…. Her eyes were closing. She could hear Nanna and Doddy talking in the front seat; their voices had a warm sound…. She thought of crackers, and a round golden orange, and a mug full of milk. But it seemed that she could not open her eyes.

When she awoke, a beautiful red and yellow wall was just outside the window of the car, and it was standing still. On the side of the wall were two babies not much older than Gwen, but many times larger, and they were eating something out of a bowl; but they seemed never to put their spoons into their mouths. Gwen smiled at them and said, "Bay-bee!" She turned to share the glory of their presence with Nanna. But

neither Nanna nor Doddy was in the front seat. Doddy was standing out in the road; he had part of the car lifted up in the air; the sun gleamed brightly on the uplifted sheet of metal, and he was prying underneath it with something that glimmered.

Nanna was across the road, standing in front of a little building. The building, too, was beautiful; it had red and white curly-cues all over it, and a delicious odor of things cooking seemed to emanate from it.

Gwen stood up and waved her arms and screamed uproariously, beating a wild tattoo on the glass with her hands. She yelled, "Nanna — Nanna — "

Her mother came back across the road; she waited for a moment until several cars had whizzed past, and then she scurried over the pavement. Gwen giggled at seeing her run.... Nanna had two round, papery things in her hand.

"Did you say mustard on yours, Joe?"

He straightened up; his face looked very wrinkly, and Gwen smiled at seeing him. "Yeh. Mustard.... Kid, I dunno what it is. Those taps seem to be all right. I dunno; maybe the rocker-arms could use a little oil. Something's sticking."

Nanna opened the door of the car and Gwen fell into her arms, still chuckling. "Here's my big girl! Are you ready for your milk?"

"Eat." Gwen reached for the round, papery things in Nanna's hand. Something smelled very appetizing.

"No, honey-bunch. Baby can't. No, no.... Gee, Joe, she's trying to get these hot dogs."

"Put 'em down on the running board — "

"No, *no*, baby.... See — here's baby's milk. In this bottle. Here, all nice — "

Gwen sat on Nanna's lap. She had a paper napkin tucked under her chin, and she drank deeply out of her own white mug. The milk filled her mouth with richness; she could have wished that it was a little warmer, but it tasted good anyway.... After a time, she pushed the cup from her and demanded, "Crackaw?"

"Joe, where'd you put those crackers?"

"Didn't have them. Yes, I did too. Down next to that straw suitcase. Next to the seat."

Nanna found the red box. Gwen yelled, "Crackaw!"

"Yes, cracker. Isn't that nice? Cracker for baby. Now, sit down there on your mattress. Good girl. Sit down."

Doddy was sitting on the running board. He had taken the paper wrapping from the round object, and he was munching gravely.

"How's your hot dog, Joe?"

"Notsa bad. I've seen better.... Makes you thirsty."

"Go across to the stand. They'll give you a drink. That lady's real nice."

"Spose she would?"

"Sure. Go on.... Take this cup, honey. Bring me a drink, too."

When he came back, he carried a brown can with a long, pointed spout, and behind him waddled a fat, rosy-faced woman with a gray sweater, and a man's old cap pulled down over her short gray hair. She laughed, "Hello there again, lady. I just hadda come over an' see baby."

Nanna held Gwen up to the open window. Doddy was poking the long spout of his can under the

uplifted part of the car. "Squeejee, squeejee, squeejee — " chanted the fat woman, squeezing Gwen's hands.

Gwen grinned at her and said, "Hay-oh."

"Ja hear that?" the fat woman chortled. "She says hello. Ain't that cute? What's her name?"

"Gwendolyn Marie…. She's nineteen months."

"She's little," said the fat woman, "but she looks like a awful healthy baby. I got two. The girl's married an' lives over at West Springs."

Gwen sniffed at the fat woman's sleeve. There was a comfortable, sweetish odor about her — the odor of fried meat and hot things in a kitchen. "I bet she smells the hamburg," beamed the visitor. "My land, I get all splashed up with that grease. You going far?"

"Burlington," replied Nanna. "Joe's got a job with the Mid-Ocean Sieve Company. If we ever get there."

"Oh. You'll make it." She muzzled down at Gwen and made a little grunting noise. Gwen laughed. The fat woman turned to Doddy. "Through with that oil, mister?"

"I oiled 'em," nodded Joe. "I'm sure much obliged. Maybe we'll have better luck now." He handed the can to the woman, and climbed into his seat. The car began to whistle and jiggle pleasantly. "By gosh," said Doddy. "That loosened her up, for now anyway. Sure much obliged."

The fat woman waved the oil can and threw a kiss to Gwen as the car pulled away. Gwen waved, "Bye," until the road was only a narrow slit behind them — until the fat woman was like a gray bug, crossing the slit.

"I bet she thought I was gonna beat it with that oil can."

"Oh, Joe! She was just being nice to baby."

"Maybe so…. That oil loosened it. It don't spit like it did. Maybe we'll make it to Burlington yet."

They drove for an eternity…. Gwen sat up on the mattress and played with her zebra. It was a rubber zebra, blown full of air. She called it, "Horshy." She twisted its ears and squealed, "Horshy, horshy!"

"Lookit, Joe."

"What?"

"She was kissing that zebra. Gee…."

He permitted himself a swift glance over his shoulder. "You oughtn't to let her chew that. It's dirty."

"She wasn't chewing it. Was you, mother's precious?"

Gwen sat up and pointed to a field which they were passing. The field was full of Moos; one of the Moos switched its tail and nodded kindly at her. "Horshy!" said Gwen.

"No, baby. That's Cow. A Moo-Cow-Moo. Say Moo."

"Horshy-moo," said Gwen, and fell over upon the mattress, much pleased with herself. She sat up and demanded, "Crackaw."

Nanna fumbled around. "Joe, I can't find that box of crackers."

"Gosh, kid! They're all gone. I ate the last one awhile ago, and threw out the box."

"Crackaw," petitioned Gwen.

"Ain't there any oranges left, Agnes?"

"She had the last orange awhile ago…. Oh, Joe, I just guess we'll have to stop and buy something. She didn't have much for her lunch. I bet she's awful hungry."

Tall weeds began to brush the glass; the wheels bounced over hummocks, and the car came to a

clattering stop. Doddy felt in his pocket and brought out a handful of bright, round things. Gwen reached for them, but he held them farther away. "Sixty-five, ninety, a dollar fifteen, a dollar twenty, a dollar twenty-two. Kid, you got any money?"

"Fifteen cents left from those hot dogs, Joe."

"That makes one-thirty-seven."

Gwen stood up and rubbed her nose against the glass; the weeds were soft and yellow, just outside. She had forgotten the cracker. She whispered, "Pretty."

"We'll have to buy five more gallons of gas, kid. At least that. And maybe oil. A quart. That'll be one-twenty-eight. That leaves nine cents. Could we get something for baby for nine cents?"

"Joe, what about our supper?"

"If you can wait, we ought to make it by eight o'clock. I'll find Harry Spevak. He'll lend me some dough. And he said he'd have a place all ready for us to step into, till we could get a house. They won't ask for rent tonight. Or maybe he's paid it."

Gwen looked out of the rear window. The sky was broken into scallops of white; they were like flowers, too. She thought of the gold flowers beside the car, the purple flowers she had seen so long before. She thought of the Wow, with its attentive ears…. "Pretty-Wow," she said quietly.

"Maybe we could stop at a store. Get crackers — graham crackers — in a sack instead of package. You know, in bulk. Then you and me could have some, too."

A car was coming from behind. Gwen watched it; maybe another Wow, a big yellow Wow, would be riding in it. The car swung from side to side, and came closer with a loud noise, but Gwen was not

frightened. Cars did not hurt you; cars were nice; only you must not grab the round wheel in Doddy's hands....

Then there was a great smash; it sounded like the time when Gwen had upset the bread-box and jelly glasses in the pantry, only much louder.... Gwen was thrown up into the air and down upon something soft; the rubber zebra struck her in the face. She snatched at its leg and cried indignantly, "Horshy!"

There was a shrill noise, very close at hand. Gwen couldn't see anything but Nanna's old coat just above her head.... She lay still and listened.

"You hurt, kid? Agnes, you — "

"No, no. Don't mind — Baby! *Gwendolyn! My honey-bunch — Joe — !*"

Something hard and broken came tinkling down beside Gwen. Maybe more jelly glasses —

Doddy was lifting her high — higher — She was in the open air; Nanna seized her. Nanna was all dusty, and there was something black and gummy on her hand. Gwen waved the zebra and cried excitedly, "Horshy — "

"Joe! She's all right, Joe! Not even crying — My baby! Baby — "

Gwen was somewhat bewildered. First flowers — and then another car came; was there a Wow in it, after all? She asked, "Crackaw?"

The other car had stopped, on the opposite side of the road somewhat ahead of them. Their own car was on its side in the ditch; yellow flowers grew up, all around it. Gwen smiled, to see it there.

Doddy had a bright red mark on his cheek. He rubbed it, and the mark became wider. He made an odd sound, and shook his head, and began to run toward the other car.

"Joe! Joe! Don't you — "

A man was climbing slowly out of the other car. He was grinning. When he stood up beside the car, he held to the open door beside him. His face was very red — redder than the fat woman's — almost as red as the mark on Doddy's face —

"Well," he said. "That was some bump."

"You almost killed us," said Doddy. "Lookit my car!"

"I see it. I see your — car. Pile of junk."

"You broke the wheel," said Doddy. "Bent that fender. Lookit it!"

"Pile of junk," said the other man. He was still grinning. He pulled a roll of paper out of his pocket. "Buy it for ten dollars."

Doddy said something — Gwen couldn't hear what it was — and began to take off his sweater. "I was clear off the pavement. You'll do time for this, you. Or — "

Gwen giggled. Nanna clutched her tightly and whispered, "Joe."

Doddy didn't turn his head. He started toward the other man. "You think just because you got a big Auburn, you can go around killing other folks — "

"Buy it for ten dollars," repeated the man with the red face. He threw two folded slips of paper down in the road, and turned around. His movements were unsteady; he trembled crazily as he climbed into his car; and Gwen laughed. "Bye," she waved.

The big car moved away from them. It began to sway from side to side. It went up over a hill, out of sight.

"Joe!" cried Nanna. "I bet he'll kill somebody! Why didn't you stop him?"

"The town's right ahead — Baxter. He'll never get through that. They'll pick him up."

"You oughta grabbed him, Joe! Our wheel's busted — "

"He had a gun in the side pocket; I could see it. He was drunk. I wasn't taking no chances." Doddy took a handkerchief out of his pocket and wiped the red mark from his face. "Ten dollars, Agnes. We're sure outa luck. That wheel'll cost — "

He stooped down and picked up the two folded slips of paper. He screamed suddenly and jumped into the air. Gwen began to clap her hands.

"Agnes! These are *fifties!* Two fifties! A hundred bucks — "

Nanna ran to him, carrying Gwen. Gwen reached for the pieces of paper. She said, "Pay-pay — " But Doddy snatched them away and waved them in the air. "We're rich, folks! By gosh — that wheel — I can get another cheap. I — "

Gwen began to sing, a song without words. She stopped and demanded, "Crackaw?"

"Yes, baby! You little skeezix! Right away — "

Other cars stopped, one from each direction. Men came climbing out. There was a little girl in a green coat. She stared at Gwen.

The men were talking with Doddy. "How'd it happen?"

"Fellow hit me. Help me lift her up, will you?"

"Sure." They all grabbed the car and hoisted it slowly up on its wheels. Doddy climbed into his seat; the suitcases and mattress were all tumbled around; but the car began to buzz and quiver. "She's all

right. Just that glass and wheel and fender — ”

“Did he stop?”

“Sure. He settled right off. A big Auburn.”

One of the men nodded. “I saw him. Turned off on Twenty-five. Going like hell; you were lucky.”

“Sure was. Thanks a lot…. You going to town?” he asked the other man.

“You bet. Give you a ride.”

Nanna took Gwen and climbed back into their own car. “I’ll wait here, Joe. Wait till you come out with the garage man.”

“All right. You wait. I’ll bring something to eat.” Doddy waved at them; his face was all wrinkled with smiles. Then the cars all made a great noise, and drove away; the little girl in the green coat was gone; and Nanna and Gwen were sitting there alone.

Nanna hummed softly, *“That was plucky Lindy’s lucky day — ”* Her hands rubbed over Gwen; they were soft, slender and warm. Gwen hugged her zebra and let her eyes go shut…. Thinking of the girl in the green coat, of Doddy gone to bring crackers, of the many cars and the man with the bright, red face.

It had, she thought, been very wonderful. She had enjoyed herself. Wow and flowers and milk. And the fat woman who smelled nice, and the odd noise when she had been thrown into the air and down again on something soft. It had been a good day, free from worry of any kind.

MANY MILES PER HOUR

We used to see him going down the highway fifty miles an hour, and my brother Mike used to look kind of sore and jealous.

There he goes, Mike used to say. Where in hell do you think he's going?

Nowhere, I guess, I used to say.

He's in a pretty big hurry for a man who's going nowhere.

I guess he's just turning her loose to see how fast she'll go.

She goes fast enough, Mike used to say. Where the hell can he go from here? Fowler, that's where. That good-for-nothing town.

Or Hanford, I used to say. Or Bakersfield. Don't forget Bakersfield, because it's on the highway. He could make it in three hours.

Two, Mike used to say. He could make it in an hour and three quarters.

Mike was twelve and I was ten, and in those days, 1918, a coupé was a funny-looking affair, an apple box on four wheels. It wasn't easy to get any kind of a car to go fifty miles an hour, let alone a

WILLIAM SAROYAN

Ford coupé, but we figured this man had fixed up the motor of his car. We figured he had made a racer out of his little yellow coupé.

We used to see the automobile every day, going down the highway toward Fowler, and an hour or so later we used to see it coming back. On the way down, the car would be travelling like a bat out of hell, rattling and shaking and bouncing, and the man in the car would be smoking a cigarette and smiling to himself, like somebody a little crazy. But on the way back, it would be going no more than ten miles an hour, and the man at the wheel would be calm and sort of slumped down, kind of tired.

He was a fellow you couldn't tell anything about. You couldn't tell how old he was, or what nationality, or anything else. He certainly wasn't more than forty, although he might be less than thirty; and he certainly wasn't Italian, Greek, Armenian, Russian, Chinese, Japanese, German, or any of the other nationalities we knew.

I figure he's an American, Mike used to say. I figure he's a salesman of some kind. He hurries down the highway to some little town and sells something, and comes back, taking it easy.

Maybe, I used to say.

But I didn't think so. I figured he was more likely to be a guy who *liked* to drive down the highway in a big hurry, just for the devil of it.

Those were the years of automobile races: Dario Resta, Jimmie Murphy, Jimmie Chevrolet, and a lot of other boys who finally got killed in racetrack accidents. Those were the days when everybody in America was getting acquainted with the idea of speed. My brother Mike often thought of getting some money somewhere and buying a second-hand car and fixing it up and making it go very fast. Sixty miles an hour maybe.

He thought that would be something to do. It was the money, though, that he didn't have.

When I buy my hack, Mike used to say, you're going to see some real speed.

You ain't going to buy no hack, I used to say. What you going to buy a hack with?

I'll get money some way, Mike used to say.

The highway passed in front of our house on Railroad Avenue, just a half-mile south of Rosenberg's Dried Fruit Packing House. Rosenberg's was four brothers who bought figs, dried peaches, apricots, nectarines, and raisins, and put them up in nice cartons and sent them all over the country, and even to foreign countries in Europe. Every summer they hired a lot of people from our part of town, and the women packed the stuff, and the men did harder work, with hand trucks. Mike went down for a job, but one of the brothers told him to wait another year till he got a little huskier.

That was better than nothing, and Mike couldn't wait to get huskier. He used to look at the pulp-paper magazines for the advertisements of guys like Lionel Strongfort and Earl Liederman, them giants of physical culture, them big guys who could lift a sack of flour over their heads with one arm, and a lot of other things. Mike used to wonder how them big guys got that way, and he used to go down to Cosmos Playground and practice chinning himself on the crossbars, and he used to do a lot of running to develop the muscles of his legs. Mike got to be pretty solid, but not much huskier than he had been. When the hot weather came Mike stopped training. It was too hot to bother.

We started sitting on the steps of our front porch, watching the cars go by. In front of the highway were the railroad tracks, and we could look north and south for miles because it was all level land. We could see a locomotive coming south from town, and we could sit on the steps of our front porch and watch it come

closer and closer, and hear it too, and then we could look south and watch it disappear. We did that all one summer during school vacation.

There goes locomotive S. P. 797, Mike used to say.

Yes, sir.

There goes Santa Fe 485321, I used to say. What do you figure is in that boxcar, Mike?

Raisins, Mike used to say. Rosenberg's raisins, or figs, or dried peaches, or apricots. Boy, I'll be glad when next summer rolls around, so I can go to work at Rosenberg's and buy me that hack.

Boy, I used to say.

Just thinking of working at Rosenberg's used to do something to Mike. He used to jump up and start shadowboxing, puffing like a professional fighter, pulling up his tights every once in a while, and grunting.

Boy.

Boy, what he was going to do at Rosenberg's.

It was hell for Mike not to have a job at Rosenberg's, making money, so he could buy his old hack and fix the motor and make it go sixty miles an hour. He used to talk about the old hack all day, sitting on the steps of the porch and watching the cars and trains go by. When the yellow Ford coupé showed up, Mike used to get a little sore, because it was fast. It made him jealous to think of that fellow in the fast car, going down the highway fifty miles an hour.

When I get my hack, Mike used to say, I'll show that guy what real speed is.

We used to walk to town every once in a while. Actually it was at least once every day, but the days were so long every day seemed like a week and it would seem like we hadn't been to town for a week, although

– 89 –

we had been there the day before. We used to walk to town, and around town, and then back home again. There was nowhere to go and nothing to do, but we used to get a kick out of walking by the garages and used-car lots on Broadway, especially Mike.

One day we saw the yellow Ford coupé in Ben Mallock's garage on Broadway, and Mike grabbed me by the arm.

There it is, Joe, he said. There's that racer. Let's go in.

We went in and stood by the car. There was no one around, and it was very quiet.

Then the man who owned the car stuck his head out from underneath the car. He looked like the happiest man in the world.

Hello, Mike said.

Howdy, boys, said the man who owned the yellow coupé.

Something wrong? said Mike.

Nothing serious, said the man. Just keeping the old boat in shape.

You don't know us, said Mike. We live in that white house on Railroad Avenue, near Walnut. We see you going down the highway every day.

Oh, yes, said the man. I thought I'd seen you boys somewhere.

My brother Mike, I said, says you're a salesman.

He's wrong, said the man.

I waited for him to tell us *what* he was, if he wasn't a salesman, but he didn't say anything.

I'm going to buy a car myself next year, said Mike. I figure I'll get me a fast Chevrolet.

He did a little shadowboxing, just thinking about the car, and then he got self-conscious, and the man busted out laughing.

Great idea, he said. Great idea.

He crawled out from under the car and lit a cigarette.

I figure you go about fifty miles an hour, said Mike.

Fifty-two to be exact, said the man. I hope to make sixty one of these days.

I could see Mike liked the fellow very much, and I knew I liked him. He was younger than we had imagined. He was probably no more than twenty-five, but he acted no older than a boy of fifteen or sixteen. We thought he was great.

Mike said, What's your name?

Mike could ask a question like that without sounding silly.

Bill, said the man. Bill Wallace. Everybody calls me Speed Wallace.

My name's Mike Flor, said Mike. I'm pleased to meet you. This is my brother Joe.

Mike and the man shook hands. Mike began to shadowbox again.

How would you boys like a little ride? Speed Wallace said.

Oh boy, said Mike.

We jumped into the yellow coupé, and Speed drove out of the garage, down Broadway, and across the railroad tracks in front of Rosenberg's where the highway began. On the highway he opened up to show us a little speed. We passed our house in no time and pretty soon we were tearing down the highway forty miles an hour, then forty-five, then fifty, and pretty soon the speedometer said fifty-one, fifty-two, fifty-

three, and the car was rattling like anything.

By the time we were going fifty-six miles an hour we were in Fowler and the man slowed the car down, then stopped. It was very hot.

How about a cold drink? he said.

We got out of the car and walked into a store. Mike drank a bottle of strawberry, and so did I, and then the man said to have another. I said no, but Mike drank another.

The man drank four bottles of strawberry.

Then we got into the car and he drove back very slowly, not more than ten miles an hour, talking all the time about the car, and how fine it was to be able to go down a highway fifty miles an hour.

Do you make money? Mike said.

Not a nickel, Speed said. But one of these days I'm going to build myself a racer and get into the County Fair races, and make some money.

Boy, said Mike.

He let us off at our house, and we talked about the ride for three hours straight.

It was swell. Speed Wallace was a great guy.

In September the County Fair opened. There was a dirt track out there, a mile around. We read advertising cards on fences that said there would be automobile races out there this year.

One day we noticed that the yellow Ford coupé hadn't gone down the highway a whole week.

Mike jumped up all of a sudden when he realized it.

That guy's in the races at the Fair, he said. Come on, let's go.

And we started running down Railroad Avenue.

It was nine in the morning and the races wouldn't begin till around two-thirty, but we ran just the same.

We had to get to the Fairgrounds early so we could sneak in. It took us an hour and a half to walk and run to the Fairgrounds, and then it took us two hours more to sneak in. We were caught twice, but finally we got in.

We climbed into the grandstand and everything looked okey-dokey. There were two racing cars on the track, one black, and the other green.

After a while the black one started going around the track. When it got around to where we were sitting we both jumped up because the guy at the wheel was the man who owned the yellow coupé. We felt swell. Boy, he went fast and made a lot of noise. And plenty of dust too, going around the corners.

The races didn't start at two-thirty, they started at three. The grandstands were full of excited people. Seven racing cars got in line. Each was cranked, and the noise they made was very loud and very exciting. Then the race started and Mike started acting like a crazy man, talking to himself, shadowboxing, and jumping around.

It was the first race, a short one, twenty miles, and Speed Wallace came in fourth.

The next race was forty miles, and Speed Wallace came in second.

The third and last race was seventy-five miles, seventy-five times around the track, and the thirtieth time around Speed Wallace got out in front, just a little way, but out in front just the same: then something went wrong, the inside front wheel of Speed Wallace's racing car busted off and the car turned a 'furious somersault, away up into the air. Everybody saw Speed Wallace fly out of the car. Everybody saw

the car smash him against the wooden fence.

Mike started running down the grandstand, to get closer. I ran after him and I could hear him swearing.

The race didn't stop, but a lot of mechanics got Speed Wallace's wrecked car out of the way, and carried Speed Wallace to an ambulance. While the other cars were going around the track for the seventieth time a man got up and told the people Speed Wallace had been instantly killed.

Holy Christ.

That fellow, Mike said, he got killed. That fellow who used to go down the highway in that yellow Ford coupé, he got killed, Joe. That fellow who gave us a ride to Fowler and bought us drinks.

When it got dark, walking home, Mike started to cry. Just a little. I could tell he was crying from the way his voice sounded. He wasn't really crying.

You remember that swell guy, Joe, he said. He was the one who got killed.

We started sitting on the steps of our front porch again, watching the cars go by, but it was sad. We knew the fellow in the yellow Ford coupé wouldn't go down the highway again. Every once in a while Mike would jump up and start shadowboxing, only it wasn't the way it used to be. He wasn't happy anymore, he was sore, and it looked like he was trying to knock hell out of something in the world that caused such a lousy thing like that to happen to a guy like Speed Wallace.

HOW IT HAPPENED

She was a writing medium. This is what she wrote: —

I can remember some things upon that evening most distinctly, and others are like some vague, broken dreams. That is what makes it so difficult to tell a connected story. I have no idea now what it was that had taken me to London and brought me back so late. It just merges into all my other visits to London. But from the time that I got out at the little country station everything is extraordinarily clear. I can live it again — every instant of it.

I remember so well walking down the platform and looking at the illuminated clock at the end which told me that it was half-past eleven. I remember also my wondering whether I could get home before midnight. Then I remember the big motor, with its glaring headlights and glitter of polished brass, waiting for me outside. It was my new thirty-horsepower Robur, which had only been delivered that day. I remember also asking Perkins, my chauffeur, how she had gone, and his saying that he thought she was excellent.

ARTHUR CONAN DOYLE

"I'll try her myself," said I, and I climbed into the driver's seat.

"The gears are not the same," said he. "Perhaps, sir, I had better drive."

"No; I should like to try her," said I.

And so we started on the five-mile drive for home.

My old car had the gears as they used always to be in notches on a bar. In this car you passed the gear lever through a gate to get on the higher ones. It was not difficult to master, and soon I thought that I understood it. It was foolish, no doubt, to begin to learn a new system in the dark, but one often does foolish things, and one has not always to pay the full price for them. I got along very well until I came to Claystall Hill. It is one of the worst hills in England, a mile and a half long and one in six in places, with three fairly sharp curves. My park gates stand at the very foot of it upon the main London road.

We were just over the brow of this hill, where the grade is steepest, when the trouble began. I had been on the top speed, and wanted to get her on the free; but she stuck between gears, and I had to get her back on the top again. By this time she was going at a great rate, so I clapped on both brakes, and one after the other they gave way. I didn't mind so much when I felt my footbrake snap, but when I put all my weight on my side brake, and the lever clanged to its full limit without a catch, it brought a cold sweat out of me. By this time we were fairly tearing down the slope. The lights were brilliant, and I brought her round the first curve all right. Then we did the second one, though it was a close shave for the ditch. There was a mile of straight then with the third curve beneath it, and after that the gate of the park. If I could shoot into that harbor all would be well, for the slope up to the house would bring her to a stand.

Perkins behaved splendidly. I should like that to be known. He was perfectly cool and alert. I had

thought at the very beginning of taking the bank, and he read my intention.

"I wouldn't do it, sir," said he. "At this pace it must go over and we should have it on the top of us."

Of course he was right. He got to the electric switch and had it off, so we were in the free; but we were still running at a fearful pace. He laid his hands on the wheel.

"I'll keep her steady," said he, "if you care to jump and chance it. We can never get round that curve. Better jump, sir."

"No," said I; "I'll stick it out. You can jump if you like."

"I'll stick it with you, sir," said he.

If it had been the old car I should have jammed the gear lever into the reverse, and seen what would happen. I expect she would have stripped her gears or smashed up somehow, but it would have been a chance. As it was, I was helpless. Perkins tried to climb across, but you couldn't do it going at that pace. The wheels were whirring like a high wind and the big body creaking and groaning with the strain. But the lights were brilliant, and one could steer to an inch. I remember thinking what an awful and yet majestic sight we should appear to anyone who met us. It was a narrow road, and we were just a great, roaring, golden death to anyone who came in our path.

We got round the corner with one wheel three feet high upon the bank. I thought we were surely over, but after staggering for a moment she righted and darted onwards. That was the third corner and the last one. There was only the park gate now. It was facing us, but, as luck would have it, not facing us directly. It was about twenty yards to the left up the main road into which we ran. Perhaps I could have done it, but I expect that the steering gear had been jarred when we ran on the bank. The wheel did not turn easily. We

shot out of the lane. I saw the open gate on the left. I whirled round my wheel with all the strength of my wrists. Perkins and I threw our bodies across, and then the next instant, going at fifty miles an hour, my right front wheel struck full on the righthand pillar of my own gate. I heard the crash. I was conscious of flying through the air, and then — and then — !

When I became aware of my own existence once more I was among some brushwood in the shadow of the oaks upon the lodge side of the drive. A man was standing beside me. I imagined at first that it was Perkins, but when I looked again I saw that it was Stanley, a man whom I had known at college some years before, and for whom I had a really genuine affection. There was always something peculiarly sympathetic to me in Stanley's personality; and I was proud to think that I had some similar influence upon him. At the present moment I was surprised to see him, but I was like a man in a dream, giddy and shaken and quite prepared to take things as I found them without questioning them.

"What a smash!" I said. "Good Lord, what an awful smash!"

He nodded his head, and even in the gloom I could see that he was smiling the gentle, wistful smile which I connected with him.

I was quite unable to move. Indeed, I had not any desire to try to move. But my senses were exceedingly alert. I saw the wreck of the motor lit up by the moving lanterns. I saw the little group of people and heard the hushed voices. There were the lodgekeeper and his wife, and one or two more. They were taking no notice of me, but were very busy round the car. Then suddenly I heard a cry of pain.

"The weight is on him. Lift it easy," cried a voice.

"It's only my leg!" said another one, which I recognized as Perkins's. "Where's master?" he cried.

"Here I am," I answered, but they did not seem to hear me. They were all bending over something which lay in front of the car.

Stanley laid his hand upon my shoulder, and his touch was inexpressibly soothing. I felt light and happy, in spite of all.

"No pain, of course?" said he.

"None," said I.

"There never is," said he.

And then suddenly a wave of amazement passed over me. Stanley! Stanley! Why, Stanley had surely died of enteric at Bloemfontein in the Boer War!

"Stanley!" I cried, and the words seemed to choke my throat — "Stanley, you are dead."

He looked at me with the same old gentle, wistful smile.

"So are you," he answered.

F. SCOTT FITZGERALD (1896–1940) rose to literary stardom early in his career. He was born in St. Paul, Minnesota, and educated at Princeton University. His glamorous private life with his celebrated wife Zelda was reflected in the characters of his many popular novels. Before his death at 44, he produced such literary classics as *This Side of Paradise* (1920), *The Beautiful and the Damned* (1922), *The Great Gatsby* (1925), and *Tender Is the Night* (1933). "The Family Bus" was written while he was living in France in 1933.

JACK FINNEY (1911–), the distinguished author of a number of novels that have become cult classics, was born in Milwaukee, Wisconsin. His literary theme tends to be an escape from the present into the idyllic past, often achieved with a light touch of science fiction. He is most recognized for *Invasion of the Body Snatchers* (1955) and the illustrated novel *Time and Again* (1979). "Second Chance" was written in 1957.

MACKINLAY KANTOR (1904–1977), one of the most prolific American writers of his time, was born in Webster City, Iowa. He worked as a newspaper reporter, columnist, screen writer, police officer, and war correspondent. Over the span of his long career he wrote numerous novels for children and stories for popular detective/crime magazines. He won an O. Henry Award for "Silent Grow the Guns" in 1935 and the Pulitzer Prize in 1956 for his novel *Andersonville.* A number of his books have been made into motion pictures including the Academy Award-winning *The Best Years of Our Lives* in 1946. "And These Went Down to Burlington" was written in 1929.

WILLIAM SAROYAN (1908–1981) was born and died in Fresno, California. His writings were romantic celebrations of American life, and his most notable novel was *The Human Comedy,* which was later made into a motion picture starring Mickey Rooney. He was a versatile author, penning plays, novels, and more than 400 short stories. The American classic "The Daring Young Man on the Flying Trapeze" won an O. Henry Award in 1934. Saroyan refused the Pulitzer Prize for his play *The Time of Your Life* on the ground that wealth and business cannot judge art. "Many Miles Per Hour" was written in 1937.

ARTHUR CONAN DOYLE (1859–1930), of Scottish descent, found international fame when he introduced the world to arch-detective Sherlock Holmes. Doyle went on to produce four novels and more than fifty stories based on the adventures of Sherlock Holmes. Later in life, about 1912, he became fascinated with spiritualism and wrote a series of stories exploring psychic phenomena. "How It Happened," written in 1913, is a story from this period.

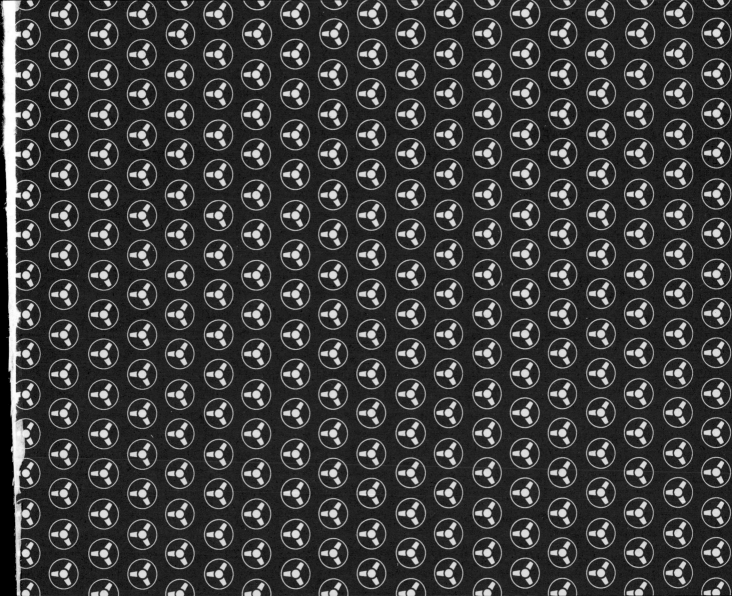

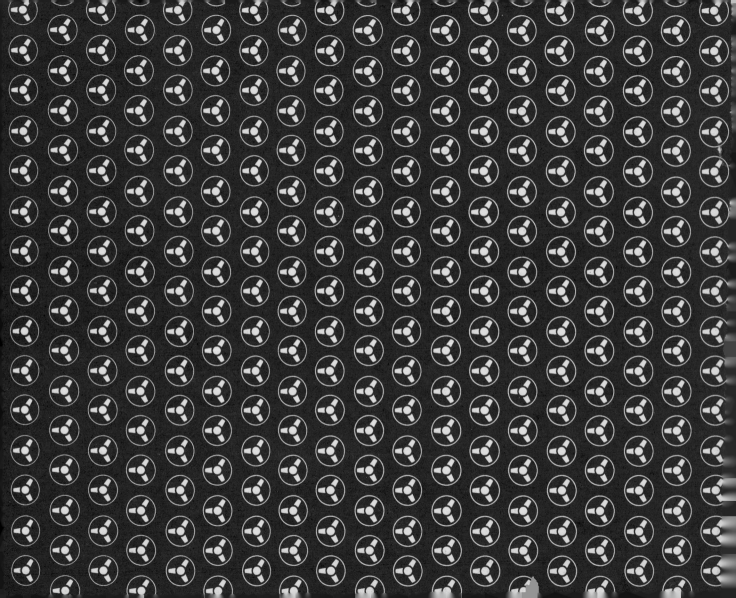